Bunty Armitage

Circus Girl

Pixi Robertson

**Bunty Armitage
Circus Girl**

First Edition
ISBN: 978-0-646-48145-6

Published 2014 - Australia

Bunty Armitage Circus Girl is a private
publication by Bounty Publishing
Available from www.lulu.com
Keywords: 'Pixi Robertson'

Dedicated to the memory of Alice Evaline (Evelyn) Hyland Coverley

Pioneering circus woman extra-ordinaire

Ev to her friends, an inspiration to many

ACKNOWLEDGEMENTS

My sincere thanks go to Evelyn Coverley (1898-2000) for her friendship and the stories on which I have based the life of Louisa Ireland, and also to Ev's family.

A big thank you and hugs to Gwen Knox, Artistic Director of Theatre Kimberly, Broome, who told me to 'just do it'; Meredith Bell, also of Theatre Kimberly; Judith Lanigan ('Miss Judith, Hula-Hoopist Supreme) who introduced me to Lulu Publishing; Dr Maggie Haertsch for her belief and *joi de vivre;* and my husband, Jimbo, for doing the washing-up and for supplying love and writing paper.

Special *merci beaucoup* to Cheryl Lee Player for lots of bubbles and makeup expertise.

A big thank you to Crystal-Burke Horton, founder of Bounty Publishing and the Queen of Can-Do.

Thank you, too, to the late and much-loved Alfie Warren, my first circus teacher and spinner of yarns and circus lore, and all the other wonderful circus folk in my life who have shared their special knowledge and stories and provided me with life-long inspiration.

Special thanks to Kerry Freeman for the use of her wonderful photographs *(The Grand Colonial Circus)* and Mark St Leon for permission to reproduce the photo on page 52 from his history of Australian circus, *Spangles & Sawdust*. If Fred Lord (*Little Big Top*) has a family out there somewhere, thank you to them, too.

Thank you also to Edith Cowan University, Bunbury, Western Australia.

Finally, thank you to the Childrens Book Council of NSW "Frustrated Writers' Awards" and James Moloney.

Chapter 1

'Okay, hold it. Now, *action.*'

I could hear the director's voice clearly through the thin walls of the caravan. I stood in the doorway and looked out at the scene before me. A group of kids, big and little, ran to their spots marked on the red earth while the cameramen and techies scurried around like a mob of ants. Welcome to the mad world of filming a television mini-series.

'Come on, Bunty, they want you in make-up.'

I ran down the steps of my dressing-room caravan and up another set of steps into the make-up van. Was this really happening to me? Had my dear, stuffy parents actually allowed me to go off on this mad adventure with a film crew, a chaperone, and no school for six months? How good is that?

I flopped into a chair and Cherry, the make-up *artiste* (as she liked to call herself), instantly began talking.

'Just look at you Bunty, all sweaty. Why can't you go a bit easy on yourself?' (On *you*, more like it, I thought.) 'I don't know, a nice kid like you, nice skin and all, why don't you look after yourself a bit more, you know, make-up and nice clothes and that?'

I disengaged my brain from Cherry's friendly but irritating chatter and tried to run over the script for the coming shoot. I couldn't concentrate. Already it was stinking hot outside and the little air-conditioner on the van was going flat out. But I couldn't complain, really. Like, who would, given this opportunity? I still couldn't believe my good luck and had to pinch myself every half hour or so, just to be sure I wasn't dreaming.

Two months earlier I was just an ordinary high school chick. You know, hanging out with girlfriends, talking about boys, doing homework, fronting up to boring old school. Boring. Most things in my life were boring yet, unknown to my friends, even my best friend Cilla, I led a secret life. I *fantasized*. I read and read and read everything I could get my hands on. I wrote stuff, plays and poems and unfinished novels and acted out the plays in my bedroom. As I lay in bed at night I visited far away countries and met fascinating men and had wild adventures.

And then the most incredible thing happened. Cilla, who is famously beautiful with blonde hair and to-die-for legs and who goes to ballet class and can sing like a bird and wants to be a 'star', showed me the fateful ad in the paper.

'Look,' she said, flopping down beside me at morning recess. 'I've just *got* to audition for *this*." She shook a newspaper in my face and I peered vaguely where she pointed. It took me a while to focus as I had been off floating in the Aegean Sea on a raft.

'Duchesse Films,' Cilla read in her very best voice, 'Principal roles, auditions on Thursday 5th, Friday 6th and Saturday 7th. To be filmed on location in Western Australia. Men blah, blah, blah, women rhubarb, rhubarb, boys etcetera. Now look, here's the exciting bit, Female lead, 14 to 18 years of age, *no experience necessary*, circus skills desirable. Must be free to travel.' Cilla's voice rose to a squeak. 'Oh, Bunty. This is just the chance I've been waiting for.' She pulled me to my feet, dancing around excitedly, hugging me and pleading, 'But you'll have to come with me, I'll be so nervous. Oh, say you'll come, per-lease?"

So I went. I held her hand (figuratively) and told her she was the most talented, most beautiful, coolest girl in the room and that the film people would be mad if they didn't pick her. Sounds like rubbish, I know, but I meant it. Cilla would really have been good, but how was I to know what was about to happen?

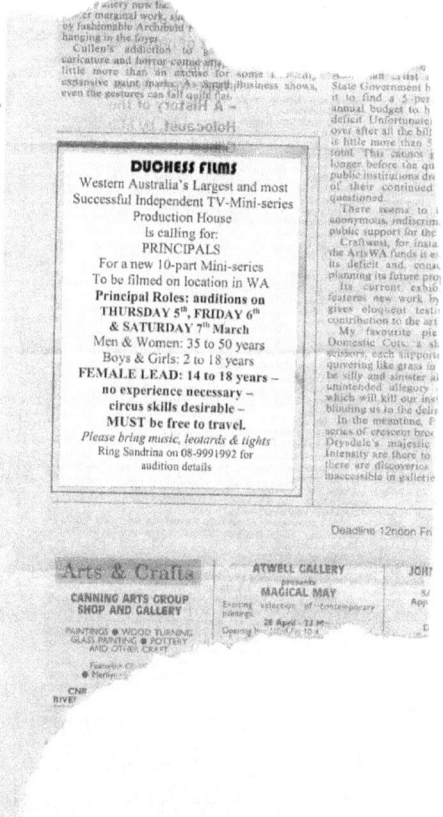

DUCHESS FILMS

Western Australia's Largest and most
Successful Independent TV-Mini-series
Production House
Is calling for:
PRINCIPALS
For a new 10-part Mini-series
To be filmed on location in WA
Principal Roles: auditions on
THURSDAY 5th, FRIDAY 6th
& SATURDAY 7th March
Men & Women: 35 to 50 years
Boys & Girls: 2 to 18 years
FEMALE LEAD: 14 to 18 years –
no experience necessary –
circus skills desirable –
MUST be free to travel.
Please bring music, leotards & tights
Ring Sandrina on 08-9991992 for
audition details

When we got to the hall where the auditions were held we had to sit for ages in a kind of waiting room packed with gorgeous girls, lots of them with their mums. What a bunch of losers. Honestly, it would have made you puke. I've never been in a room full of such self-centered, under-fed egotists before, and I *never* want to repeat the experience. You wouldn't believe the amount of hair-fluffing and lip-pouting and looking in mirrors that went on. Compared to this lot Cilla, who I always thought was the last word in vain, was the essence of modesty.

We sat in that horrible place for hours and eventually they called Cilla. Everybody else had gone by that time and I sat there biting my nails in agony, wondering what kind of tortures they were putting my poor friend through. I couldn't imagine how humiliating it would be to get up in front of a bunch of strangers and try to convince them that you were the one-and-only star they had been searching for.

After about a year and a half Cilla came back. She looked like a limp rag. Her hair was flat and sweaty and her make-up was decidedly the worse for wear. Poor thing. She sank on to the seat beside me.

'How'd you go?' I whispered, dying to know but scared, too, for her.

'Dunno,' she replied in a little voice. So un-Cilla, usually so confident, so sure of herself.

'Well …?'

'Well, they haven't made a decision yet. They'll let me know, the old "Don't ring us, we'll ring you" rubbish.'

I was terrified my friend would burst into tears. How embarrassing. I grabbed her arm. I had to get her somewhere she could pull herself together. I can tell you it's pretty unnerving when your best friend looks like having a nervous breakdown in public.

We were halfway to the exit when the door to the audition room flew open. A large, I mean *very* large, man appeared and stared as we crossed the wooden floor, Cilla click-clacking all the way in her ridiculously high heels.

'Where do you think you're going?'

We turned to stare at the man.

'Who, us?' I managed to squeeze out.

'No, no. You darling, just you."

He sounded like one of those English actors you see on old black and white movies.

And then I realised he was pointing at me, not Cilla. I pointed at myself.

'Yes, yes, you. Do hurry, we've not got all day, y' know. Now, do come along.' He turned back into the audition room.

I looked at Cilla. Cilla looked at me. She turned towards the exit door leaving me stuck to the spot. I stared helplessly at her back, then at the other door. I could feel myself stretching in two directions.

The man called again. The door slammed behind Cilla's back as I turned and walked into the other room. What was I doing?

Chapter 2

'Bunty, you're wanted on set!'

'There you go Love, all fixed.' Cherry gave my face a final swoosh of powder, dabbed the loose stuff away, and shooed me out of the chair.

I raced out of the make-up van and down into the dust where Tim, "The Boss", stood talking and waving his arms around like a madman. The poor camera man kept opening his mouth to speak but never seemed to get any words out. O-oh, The Boss is in a good mood – not. Best steer clear, I thought, and quietly took up my place where the next scene would begin.

While I stood and sweated on my mark for a good eighteen months or so, The Boss and the cameraman continued their marathon gabfest. All around me the extras sweated, too, and the horses stamped their impatient hooves. It was a very hot day in Meekatharra. If this is winter, what would it be like in summer?

Another hundred years or so passed while The Boss walked over to the beach umbrella where Damian Duchesne sat with his mum. I could hear Mr Duchesne's deep voice rolling around and around the set but I couldn't make out what he was saying. Sometimes you can be looking at somebody while they talk to you, but you don't hear a word. Your ears just sort of tune out. When it happens to me I know I get this stupid look on my face, but I can't seem to do anything about it. If I don't like what's happening I can just wish myself away. I should have wished myself away that day at the audition. Then I'd still be friends with Cilla. But if I had, I wouldn't be here. So what happened? Did I trade my best friend for the chance to be a television star?

On that wonderful, dreadful day when I followed Damian Duchesne's retreating figure into the audition room, I felt like I was in one of my daydreams. I could decide when and if I went, if I should stay, if I should go, but his rich, mysterious voice drew me forward and I didn't go. Instead I stayed and played their games.

Mr Duchesne, who was then just a nameless voice, sat at a long table with three other men and two women. They looked at me as I hovered near the door. Suddenly a row of bright lights came on, dazzling me. I suppose I should have felt intimidated, but I didn't. Instead I stood up straighter with my feet apart, put my hands on my hips and looked down my long nose at the blurry figures on the other side of the light. I'm a bit short-sighted, actually, so they weren't to know I was just trying not to squint. My teachers complain about this habit of mine. They say I'm arrogant and defiant. I assume it makes me look aristocratic. Well, I figure if I can't be beautiful like Cilla I may as well look interesting.

So, there we were. Me looking arrogant or aristocratic (take your pick) on one side of the table and them sitting solemn-faced on the other. *I imagined I was the Countess Irina, a desperate spy, being interrogated by her ruthless enemies. The lights bored into her eyes. Their leader spat out a command.*

"What is your name?"
"Where did you train?"
"Who is your agent?"
"How old are you?"

Wait a minute. That's a strange thing to ask a glamorous spy....

... I came back to reality with a jolt and in my best voice replied,

'Annabel Armitage. Huh? What? Sixteen,' and, 'Can I go now?' You'll have to agree I'm pretty quick-witted.

'Go? What do you mean, go? The audition is just beginning.' The large man's voice rumbled around the cavernous space.

'Audition? Oh, you want *me* to audition.' I looked around vaguely. What was I doing here?

'Look, Tim, Damian, I think we should go gently for the moment.' The speaker was one of the women at the table. I couldn't really see her but she sounded nice. Down to earth, not all plum-in-the-mouth like the large one or sarcastic like one of the other men. She stood up and walked around the end of the table, her hand held out to me. I shook her hand, surprised. Kids don't do that where I live.

'I'm Kitty Lambert. I think there's been some kind of mistake here, but don't worry, we really would like you to audition.' She turned to face the table. 'Kill those lights, guys, Miss Armitage needs a bit of space.'

Miss Armitage – wow!

The room went dim and I could see by a few overhead lights just what kind of a room I was in. It was a large hall with a wooden floor and a stage at the other end. The entire middle section was chock-a-block with all sorts of weird stuff – unicycles, juggling clubs, hoops, piles of thick plastic plates, hats, gym mats and other things I didn't recognise. Hanging from the beams of the ceiling were ropes and ladders and a real trapeze. I remembered then that the ad in the paper had said something about circus skills. Things suddenly looked decidedly interesting.

The other woman and the men remained seated, talking quietly amongst themselves, but Kitty Lambert took me by the arm and guided me down the length of the hall, stepping casually over and around various bits and pieces of strange equipment.

'Look, Annabel ...'

I interrupted, 'Call me Bunty, all my friends do.' Blabber-mouth.

'Okay. Bunty it is. Do you know what this audition is all about?'

'N – not really. I just came to keep my friend company.'

'Duchess Films is making a mini-series based on the life of Louisa Ireland who was a famous West Australian circus performer. Damian, that's Mr Duchesne who owns the film company, would like you to audition.'

She pointed at the large man. I stared blankly at her. 'Yes, Mr Duchesne thinks you have a certain physical resemblance to our film heroine.' As if. She paused, looking intently at me. 'What d' you think?'

Before I could put my brain into gear I heard myself say, 'A circus girl? All right!'

Chapter 3

The cry of 'Whale! Whale! Thar she blows, on the starb'd side!' rang out. The passengers on deck who were "taking the air" and trying to recover from the buffeting of the Great Australian Bight, rushed to the side of the sailing ship. A group of boisterous children elbowed their way to the rails. Their voices, shrill with excitement, rose up and mingled with the screams of the seagulls that swooped around the masts and rigging.

Louisa Ireland stood on tiptoe and peered over the heads of her young brothers and sisters. 'Oh, my goodness,' she breathed to herself. 'Whales!'

The giants frolicked and splashed in the wake of the vessel, leaping into the bright morning light, plunging down again to the depths of the icy ocean. She hugged herself with excitement. The little ship had been at sea for three days since leaving Adelaide and Louisa had almost given up hope of seeing these wondrous beasts. Now, here they were, performing for the delight of the passengers.

'Look, Lu, look at 'em go. We could put them in the circus if we had a big enough tank. Don't they just love showing off.' Queenie put her arm around Louisa's waist and gave her big sister a happy squeeze. 'Gosh, I was beginning to think we wouldn't

see any whales before we got to Albany. And now, just look at 'em. This beats having to practice, doesn't it?'

'Certainly is exciting, Queenie, but I think we should do some more bending practice for our contortion act anyway. You know how particular Ma is about that, and those lazy boys really do need to do a bit more juggling.'

'Aw, come on Lu, give the kids a break. You work them harder than Pa.' A tall, handsome lad moved over to the two girls and put his hand on Louisa's head, tousling her wild black curls affectionately.

She looked up at him and sighed, 'Maybe you're right, Perry, but I think Papa has enough to worry about without chasing after us all the time to practice. And as for Mama, she already has too much to do.'

'I thought this was going to be a bit of a holiday.'

'Oh, Perry. You know very well that circus people can never really have a holiday. It doesn't take long at all to get out of condition, and then where would you be? Next time we showed the circus we'd be dropping juggling clubs, and missing tricks, and grunting and groaning with the effort of tumbling and bending. Before you knew it, we would be losing audiences. Who wants to see a circus without skill, a circus of mistakes?'

'It's all right, Sis, keep your wig on.' Perry gave her hair another affectionate rub and moved off casually, calling to a boy on the opposite side of the deck.

Perry had the knack of making friends wherever he went. No sooner was the family on board ship than he'd chummed up with a lad of his own age. Alfie, a redheaded orphan on his way to live with relatives in Albany, was clearly intrigued by the circus folk he found among his fellow passengers,

'Maybe he's right.' Louisa spoke half to herself, half to her sister, as Perry and Alfie sauntered off. Her gaze was still fixed on the whales, but her mind was elsewhere.

From earliest childhood Louisa had performed in the ring of her parents travelling show, Ireland's Circus. As the eldest girl in a family of nine she had many duties outside the circus ring; helping her mother with the cooking and washing, minding the little children and seeing to their schooling, sewing costumes and practising new acts, not to mention helping with the horses and ponies. The list seemed endless.

It was in the circus ring though, that she was happiest. "Miss Louisa" walked the tight-wire, swung on a trapeze, danced on a resin-back horse, tumbled in the acrobatic acts and played a tenor horn in the band. She could also fill in for other members of the family

21

on the rare occasion when somebody was ill. And in between times there was the never-ending practice, practice, practice.

It was a heavy burden but to Lu, as her family called her, it was the only life she knew. Born "under canvas" somewhere in the outback of New South Wales, Louisa, although only fourteen, had already travelled all over the colony, and the little family circus had just returned from a two year tour of New Zealand. For Louisa, a life spent travelling the open road at the whim of her father's unerring "nose" for a "good circus town" was better than any she might have had in a sleepy country village or a crowded, squalid city.

Upon returning to Australia, Ireland's Circus toured the small, dusty wheat-belt towns of South Australia. Then, after a successful season in Adelaide, Mr Ireland decided that Western Australia was the place to be. Gold fever had struck and people were flocking to the goldfields from the other colonies, from Europe, and from California.

'Where there's gold fever there's bound to be good pickings for a circus. Let's pack up, Mama, and head for the West.'

Mr Ireland, as his family well knew, was never wrong. Within the week they were on board ship and sailing West towards the setting sun.

And so began the new adventure.

Chapter 4

'Cut! Cut! Cut!' The Boss threw his hat on the ground and wiped his arm over his sweating brow. It was hard to know, sometimes, when The Boss was pleased with a shoot, or really teed off. 'Okay, gang. Let's wrap this one. I reckon it's tucker time.'

I think he was pleased.

I reckoned it was tucker time, too. A morning spent chasing after a run-away horse and cart in the heat and dust of a little bush town was enough to give any girl a humungous appetite. The extras all went off in one direction, and the cast and crew descended like a mob of blowies on the luxurious feast outside the catering van. Goodness knows what the extras were fed, but, hey, were we treated to some absolutely wicked eats! Trestle tables groaned with fresh salads, fruit, hot pasta dishes, cold meats, home-baked bread, fresh fruit juice ... yum-oh. Film stars are supposed to be skinny. Not me.

I sat under one of the beach umbrellas propped over the café tables spread around the catering area, shoveling food into my mouth in a decidedly unladylike manner. The Boss sauntered over.

'D' you mind?' he asked, pointing at the other seat.

'No, no. 'Scuse the mouthful.' I gulped down some orange juice and cleared my throat. 'Everything okay? Are we on schedule?'

'Yeah, everything's fine. But if that bloody horse had behaved itself this morning I'd probably be feeling a little less stressed.'

'You! I was the one who had to chase the steamin' thing.'

Excuse me? Is this me talking to The Boss, this volatile man who totally over-awed me the first time we met? I mean, people who make movies and mini-series are from another planet. They are more mysterious (and kind of scarier) than your actual stars. Film stars and televisions stars, well, they're the people you see, you sort of feel you know who they are. They're in your face, in your lounge room, every day. But since being on the set I'd realised that the most important people for me are the directors and writers, the creative ones with cool imaginations and the drive to get things done. Totally awesome.

As I looked at The Boss's face talking away in the brilliant sunshine, I did a kind of mental "slow fade" to the cool, quiet of the audition. I saw The Boss sitting at the long table, waving his arms in that now familiar fashion, talking quietly but excitedly to the fat man, Damian Duchesne. Kitty Lambert was talking at me. I looked with fascination as her lips moved, certain she must be saying something, unable to concentrate.

' ... so if you can climb the rope and grab hold of the trapeze, we can see how strong you are.'

'What? Oh, sure.'

But what else had she been saying? Come on, Bunty, snap out of it. For once you are really in an adventure, so you'd better make the most of it. I looked at the rope hanging from the ceiling. I looked at the trapeze dangling up there beside it. It was a long way to the top of the hall. Suddenly I knew why I had spent all those years climbing trees, swinging off monkey-bars and messing around in the gym at school, pretending I was a star of the Moscow Circus or one of the "Flying Ashtons": *I wasn't frightened of heights and I just loved climbing.*

Up I went; hand over hand, my legs wrapped around the rope. I reached over and grabbed the bar.

'Now, do a chin up.'

'Huh?' I looked down at Kitty Lambert. Her white face, a small dot in the dark hall, peered up at me.

'Chin the bar. No, no, not like that. Turn your hands around so they face away from you. That's it; now see how many you can do.'

Normally, with my hands facing towards my body, I can do fourteen, fifteen or more chin ups, easy. But now, with my hands turned away, I suddenly felt as weak as a kitten. I was struggling to do seven of the wretched things. Totally wrecked, I swung my legs up over the bar of the trapeze, rested for a couple of seconds, then swung down to tuck my toes over the bar. Smoothly I lowered my body, doing the old toe hang I'd taught myself on the rotary clothes hoist at home. Quite relaxing, really, after the chin ups. I flexed my arms to ease the tired muscles.

'*Bunty! What the hell do you think you're doing?*'

I looked down at Kitty Lambert. She was jumping up and down, screaming, and

waving her arms around. Talk about steamin'.
There seemed to be an awful lot of arm
waving around here. Must be these
temperamental artistic types. I angled my
body around and grabbed the rope, then
swung off the trapeze and climbed down,
hand over hand. I landed on the mat with a
little thud.

Kitty Lambert was eyeballing me.
'You-could-have-killed-yourself-where-did-
you-learn-to-do-that-what-the-heck-do-you-
think-you're-playing-at-you-little-idiot?'

O-oh. I think she was impressed –
not. And I don't think she really believed me
when I told her about the clothes hoist. 'But,'
I said, 'I don't do it all the time 'cos Mum says
it's not ladylike and I can only practise when
she's not around ....' I stopped, major
embarrassment. I didn't know where to look.
I certainly didn't want to look at the rest of
the "Musketeers" who were now standing
around gawking at me.

They all began talking at once. *Where?*
What? Who? How? Seven chin ups, seven, I counted
them! The only one not talking was Kitty
Lambert. She was just staring at me, this great,
big, dorky smile on her face. She kept on
smiling and shaking her head.

After that, it was plain sailing. I had the job, they said (Job? What job?), but now they wanted me to run through a few other things. I still didn't have a clue what was going on, but I spent the next two hours being put through a grueling kind of obstacle course. Bending over this, jumping over that, walking on (falling off) a tight-wire, rolling on the mats, trying to juggle (I was pretty hopeless at that, I can tell you). Then I had to read some lines from a script. Thanks to all my practise in the bedroom I think I handled that all right, but I'm not too sure about the other bits. Oh, and I totally bombed out on the unicycle.

Kitty, who turned out to be the "circus skills co-ordinator", came to me after all this and, still with that silly smile on her face said, 'Bunty, are you *sure* you've never done any circus work before? I've never seen anyone with such natural ability, and I've certainly never seen any girl of your age – did you say you were sixteen? – I've never seen a sixteen year old girl with such power-for-weight strength. You might have been born on a circus. Guys,' she turned to the rest of the group, "I don't think there's any doubt. Bunty is definitely the girl you need. It's like

Louisa Ireland has come back to life. You must use her.'

Kitty Lambert squeezed my arm. She was pretty cool. The rest of the gang looked at me, silly smiles on their faces, too. Then they all shook my hand. Wicked.

Chapter 5

I looked down at the script in my hand and read the lines out loud:

"*Person holding* LOUISA *is revealed as* ALFIE. LOUISA *opens her eyes, gazing up at him. A tremor of excitement passes between them.* LOUISA *struggles from* ALFIE's *arms and runs to side of ship.* (LOUISA's p.o.v.) *In the wake of the speeding vessel three horses can be seen, tossed and distressed in the violent sea, frantically swimming after the receding ship. Close-up of* LOUISA, *face streaked with tears, rain and blood.*"

My stomach tightened with dread as I re-read the note that Mr Duchesne had scrawled across the bottom of the page:

Brian –
Love this, but I want Louisa to go over-board with the horses. I see her on a white stallion – thrashing through the waves in the light of a

full silver moon, wet hair streaming out behind her, foam flying on the wind ... she saves the horses (of course).

Will need to talk to horse wrangler re this.

Thanks, Damian.

I looked up at The Boss. 'I get washed overboard? Sounds scary.'

'Think you can do it?'

'W-e-ll, I guess so. But what does "v.o." mean, and what's a "p.o.v? And what's this "ext" and "int" stuff that's all over the script?'

The Boss gave a snorty laugh. 'Simple, "v.o." stands for "voice over". You can see how it'd work in Scene Twelve. We have a few set shots of the ship and the beginning of the storm and then we'd put your voice, that is, Louisa's voice, over the top of the visuals.

'Oh, right.'

'And then, "p.o.v." is just the "point of view" of a particular character – in effect what the character is seeing is also what the camera is "seeing" at that particular time. "Ext" is just short for exterior and ...'

'... and "int" is short for interior,' I said, beating him to the explanation.

'Right.'

I went back to studying the revised script.

LOUISA (v.o.)
I thought I'd die that day we lost my horse, *Merriweather*, overboard in the storm.
After the sunshine and the leaping whales, the promise of the Port of Albany lying just over the horizon made our hearts sing with happiness.
The storm came from nowhere on our last day at sea. One minute, evening calm. The next minute, the sea a boiling mass, the wind tearing at the sails.
And the horses, the poor horses, penned on deck and mad with fear.

SCENE 12.   EXT. DECK OF SAILING SHIP. TWILIGHT.
Groups of passengers dressed in Victorian-era clothes stroll the deck. On the stern can be glimpsed a large wooden pen containing horses and ponies. The sea is calm, the wind steady. A group of children in tattered pink tights and old, faded acrobatic clothes is practising a contortion act. A couple of

older boys juggle clubs off to the side.
Muted shouts of sailors going about their
every-day chores.

SCENE 13. INT. SHIP'S CABIN.
TWILIGHT.
Woman, in her forties, tends small children,
dressing and bedding them for the night.
Lamp slung from ceiling is suddenly flung
sideways, floor tilts steeply, woman
staggers. Noise of furniture, etc., falling and
crashing. Lamp is extinguished, children
begin crying.

SCENE 14. EXT. DECK OF SAILING
SHIP. TWILIGHT.
Wind howls, sails flap madly, clouds scud
across sky. People on deck run for shelter
as lightning flashes and thunder cracks.
Horses in pen begin milling about and
neighing, rearing in frenzy and fear.

SCENE 15. EXT. DECK OF SAILING
SHIIP. NIGHT.
Waves wash over deck as sailors fight to
keep sails intact and ship on course. Much
yelling of commands and directives. Extra-
large wave washes over deck and the
wooden pen splinters. Horses and water
pour out over the deck. Figures in

waterproofs lunge for horses' headstalls and confusion reigns as they fight to keep control of the animals.

LOUISA grabs at a rearing horse, her favourite. Its hoof smashes down on the side of her head, knocking her to the deck. Another wave engulfs the ship and washes the horse overboard.

SCENE 16. EXT. OCEAN. NIGHT.
(LOUISA's p.o.v.) Mountainous seas lit by full moon shining through racing storm clouds. Horse's head glimpsed over the top of waves.

SCENE 17. EXT. DECK OF SAILING SHIP. NIGHT.
LOUISA picks up rope from deck, ties one end to the mast, then loops other end around her shoulder. She dives overboard. Behind her crew and passengers can be seen staring, shouting at her, telling her to come back, not to be a fool.

SCENE 18. EXT. UNDERWATER. NIGHT.
LOUISA is seen swimming underwater amongst the churning hooves of the panicking horse, shedding her wet weather gear as she rises to the surface.

SCENE 19. EXT. OCEAN. NIGHT.
(LOUISA's p.o.v.) *She sees the horse swimming further away from her as waves continually wash over her face. Bravely she swims on. She can just make out the head of* Merriweather *over the surging water.*

SCENE 20. EXT. OCEAN. NIGHT.
LOUISA *swims to side of the horse, clambers onto its back and talks into its ear to calm it down. She gains control of the horse and with the aid of the rope turns its head towards the ship and urges it onwards.*

SCENE 21. EXT. OCEAN. NIGHT.
(LOUISA's p.o.v.) *The ship seems to be sailing off into the distance, leaving* LOUISA *and the horse in its wake.*
Cut to close-up *of* LOUISA *and look of horror on her face.*
(LOUISA's p.o.v.) *It gradually becomes apparent that the ship is actually turning in a slow arc and sailing back towards* LOUISA.

SCENE 22. EXT. SAILING SHIP. NIGHT.
Passengers and crew line the sides of the ship. The crowd erupts into cheers as they spy LOUISA *safe on the back of the horse. Improvised slings are thrown overboard*

amidst much shouting of orders and bustle on deck.
Close-up of ALFIE's *smiling face.*

SCENE 23. EXT. SAILING SHIP. DAWN.
The first rays of dawn appear as LOUISA *and the horse are winched aboard.* Medium shot *of* LOUISA *wrapped in a blanket, drinking hot tea, and being fussed over by* MRS IRELAND. *In background* MR IRELAND, PERRY, ALFIE, ARTIE *and* MICKEY *tend to the horses.*

SCENE 24. EXT. SAILING SHIP. DAWN.
LOUISA *stands beside repaired horse pen, stroking neck of* MERRIWEATHER, *the horse she rode to safety. The sky brightens behind her, the wind whips her hair.* ALFIE *appears close beside her and places his hand on the horse's neck next to her hand.* Medium shot *of the two young people as they turn to face each other.*
FADE TO BLACK.

Chapter 6

'I don't believe it. How could you do this to me? I thought you were my friend, my best friend. I'm supposed to be the star!' Cilla stopped screaming for a moment and started crying again.

I wanted to hit her, to shake her until she stopped. I felt so miserable and depressed and guilty. All I wanted was to feel happy. I put my arms around her and wiped her eyes. She pushed me away. We sat on her bed and Cilla started shredding tissues. She wouldn't look at me.

'Cilla?' I tried, tentatively.

'Oo-erg, hrmph.' Cilla stood up and flounced to the mirror. She peered at her faultless face. Even crying couldn't make her look less than gorgeous. Anxiously she patted her cheeks with some gunk and checked her eyes for redness. Nix, of course. I wished I could hate her, and then I mightn't feel so bad.

I tried again. 'Cilla ...?'

'Go away, just go away!' My ex-best friend turned and lobbed a hairbrush at me.

I went.

Cilla and I didn't speak to each other for weeks. Then she flew off to Japan with her mum and the next thing I know, a postcard arrives, written in her usual cheerful, nutty way. She drives me mad, but I can't help loving her. I guess that's the good thing about real friends, you know their faults but in the end it doesn't seem to matter.

Hi Doll Face,
 Miss you miss you
miss you.
 Japan is <u>Divine</u>!
 Shopping is unreal!
  Love, love, love,
       Cilla

XXX

Miss Bunty Armitag
2 Swan Cres
Outridge
Perth
  WA
 Australia

After Cilla arrived home from her holiday we slipped easily back into our old friendship. The exciting thing, now, was that Cilla began to get a lot of modelling bookings and her career took off in a big way. Her parents hired a local models' agent, but even more exciting for Cilla was the number of overseas, seriously big time agents who kept ringing her up with fabulous offers of work.

Now we both had something exciting to look forward to. And the best thing was that suddenly Cilla wasn't jealous any longer. In fact, she even seemed to be proud of me.

Life was looking really good.

Chapter 7

I looked at myself in the mirror. I bent my arms upwards and flexed my biceps like a strong-man. Then I turned side-ways and smoothed the heavy cotton leotard over my chest and buttocks. Get real, Bunty, you'll soon be as vain as those poor dorks at the audition.

Under the sequined costume I was covered from neck to toe in a truly hideous, hand-knitted, sick-coloured, itchy, pink jumpsuit. The wardrobe chicks told me this garment of extreme torture was known in the old days as "fleshings" and was worn to protect the virtue of the circus girls - in their dreams - and to protect the females in the audience from being offended. As if.

I turned to face my image again. I poked out my tongue and screwed up my face. The face in the mirror obligingly poked its tongue out, too. The face was brown and healthy-looking from these past few weeks spent charging all over the countryside as we madly filmed in the winter sunshine. I squinted at my reflection.

I did a "double take". I could have sworn my reflection winked at me. Na. Must be the funny light in the wardrobe van. I moved closer to the mirror and peered through the dust on its surface. The face before me moved in a kind of shimmery way. I felt hot and flushed. The heavy woollen fleshings dug into my skin and I pulled at the neckline, desperate to get the material away from my body.

I squirmed and wrenched and tugged. The sweat ran down my face and I could feel the crotch of the costume sticky between my legs. My back was sodden. My throat was stuffed with fur. I thought I was going to faint.

The face in the mirror continued to watch me, cool, calm and immobile.

'... off, I've got to get this off.' I collapsed into a chair and Mrs Blainey, the wardrobe mistress, rushed to my side.

'Oh, you poor little pet, here, let me help, what's wrong, oh dear, oh dear, there we go.' Mrs Blainey, who really was a nice old duck, fussed around and helped me out of the costume. 'Just look at this, well I never, you could wring the sweat out of these fleshings, so you could, whatever's come over you,

you're drenched, oh dear ....' She never seemed to pause for breath. I sometimes wondered if she actually needed to breathe.

'Nothing, nothing's wrong.' I didn't want to think about the face in the mirror. 'I guess, um, it was just these icky fleshings. I can't stand the feeling. It was like being inside a smelly old bear, or something.' I shuddered. The heat seemed to go out of the day.

'Well, never mind, dearie, I'm sure if I have a word with Mr Duchesne we'll be able to work something out even though he wants things to be really authentic, well, as far as possible. Did you know,' she continued on, as relentless as a steam train, 'did you know that these fleshings and leotard are the original costume worn by Louisa Ireland herself when the family first came to the West? Oh yes, there's lots of history tied up here.' Mrs Blainey sighed contentedly to herself. She just loves her costumes.

And I just loved Mrs Blainey two days later when she brought me a new set of fleshings. Mr Duchesne and Mrs Blainey worked it out between them. The new part of the costume was made from a wonderful, thoroughly modern cotton and lycra blend, so authentic-looking you could hardly tell the difference. Excellent.

But I still had to wear the original cotton leotard. Yuck. This costume was really quite strange to look at, if you're looking back at it from the end of the 20th Century as I was. Made, as I said, from stiff and unyielding cotton, it looked like it would be almost impossible to move in. How would I go wearing it on the trapeze? Those old-time circus performers sure did it tough.

The bodice of the leotard was of faded blue with red and silver sequins sewn all over it in a kind of floral pattern. The neck-line was scalloped and thin blue straps ran over each shoulder. A faded red rose was pinned high on one side. Around the hips a puffy arrangement of red velvet and blue cotton stripes stuck out all around and the leg-holes were cut low on the upper thigh. A pair of red leather lace-up boots with soft soles completed the outfit.

I told Mrs Blainey that I thought it was glamorous – not. I think she was impressed – not.

Chapter 8

'Now ... hup!' Mr Ireland's voice echoed in the morning stillness. The only other sounds were the thud of a horse's hooves as it snorted around the circus ring, and tiny grunts of exertion as Louisa swung herself up on to the cantering animal.

'Got it – good girl.'

Louisa glowed with pride at her father's praise. He cracked his whip in excitement and gestured for her to do the trick again. Down to the sawdust track she went, dismounting with careless ease. And then the drill began afresh.

Louisa stood in the middle of the ring at her father's side as he guided the horse with expert flourishes of his whip around and around the tiny space. When her father shouted 'Go!' she ran to intercept the cantering resin-back horse. Her mind drifted off for a moment as she wondered if there was enough resin on her horse's rump. Resin, the dried sap of a certain type of pine tree, was used to stop the rider's feet from slipping off the horse's shiny coat. Because of this, all circus horses used for bare-back riding were generally known as resin-backs.

With a little jolt, Louisa pulled her thoughts back to the trick she was about to try again. Her hands reached out to grasp the leather roller harness *fastened around the horse's girth and her eyes automatically fixed on the movement of the animal's front leg. Horse and panting girl ran together, step for step. Louisa pushed her shoulder against the sweating shoulder of the pony, waiting for the perfect timing.*

Now she saw it, felt it, a fraction of a second before her father's anticipated shout. Her two feet pounded forward and she swung her legs in a scissor kick. As Louisa became air-borne she twisted her torso, reversing direction to face the resin-back's rump. Laughing gaily she landed neatly astride the horse's neck, waved and blew kisses to her delighted father.

'Enough time for all that during the show, Louisa. We've got more work to do. Now, I want you, Mickey, to vault on so you're facing Lu on Bunyip's *neck. Next I want Queenie, then Artie and then Winnie up. You're going to be a bit squashed, so make sure as you land that you pull yourself in tightly behind the body in front. Mickey, tuck your legs in for a bit of leverage until everybody's on board, and then I want to see all legs straight out, pointing forwards with* POINTED TOES!'

Mr Ireland turned and glared at Artie as he said this. Artie struck a pose like a ballet dancer, and the children collapsed in a heap of laughter. Mr Ireland ignored his son as best he could and continued with the new instructions.

47

'Now, Perry, once everybody is on board, I want you to do the Jingles.'

'Oh, not that old stuff,' Perry groaned. The Jingles required a clown rider to chase the horse until he could grab its tail. Then, using the tail as leverage, the acrobat performs a series of running forward somersaults and ends with the rider astride the tail, riding it like a hobbyhorse. Audiences loved it. Perry hated it.

'Look, Perry, just because you think the Jingles is old-fashioned doesn't mean it's not worth doing any more. Like as not there are hundreds, just hundreds of youngsters in Albany who've never seen it. They will love it.' Mr Ireland gestured for his children to resume their places in the ring. Satisfied, he set the good-natured horse once more to cantering gently around the ring.

Inside the little circus tent the golden sawdust rose lazily into the air. The smell of the tan bark and the sweating horse, the shouts of the children and their father, the sound of hoof beats and the crack of the whip, blended into one perfect, glorious whole.

Louisa's heart filled with joy. For the first time since the awful storm at sea when they nearly lost Merriweather, she felt happy again.

Chapter 9

You know that feeling, déjà vu? Well, I'd been déjà vu-ing all over the place. In fact, ever since the day at the audition. I just sort of "knew" a whole lot of stuff that Kitty Lambert set out to teach me in the weeks before we began filming. It was weird, really.

As Kitty remarked, I was pretty strong for a girl and once I'd gotten over my surprise at the way things were working out I found that doing tricks on the trapeze, for instance, just seemed to come naturally. I don't know who was more freaked, Kitty or me, but the more I learnt, the more I seemed to know. My body developed a mind of its own and often just seemed to go off and do its own little thing. Muscle memory, I think it's called, but the strange thing is I had no idea where this memory came from.

Then the Boss showed me a photograph of Louisa Ireland and I totally lost it.

'Where'd you get this photo?' My voice was so squeaky with surprise I sounded like Cilla on a bad day. 'It looks like me at a fancy dress ball, or something.' I peered closely at the faded brown and white snap. 'Is this some kind of joke? I know, it's one of those computer enhancements, isn't it? You've scanned a picture of me and played around with it. Haven't you ...?' My voice faded away as I continued to gaze at the photo.

It was no joke. Louisa Ireland gazed back at me, solemnly, coolly, a faint smile dancing in her eyes. My eyes. Her mouth – my mouth. Her wild, curly dark hair. My wild, curly dark hair.

I felt a chill up my spine. No wonder I got the job. But, if I only got the job because Louisa and I looked so much alike, how come I felt so totally at home with all this circus stuff I was learning? Talk about the *X-Files!*

I remembered Kitty telling me that Mr Duchesne thought I bore a "certain physical resemblance to our film heroine". I know I've got a really wild imagination, and I know I've spent years daydreaming my young life away, but underneath it all I'm basically such a practical sort of person that this all seemed much too strange for my liking. So, I had to ask myself, did it really matter that such a happy co-incidence had got me the part in the mini-series? I couldn't make up my mind.

My folks were really supportive in their usual boring way and thought it an "excellent opportunity", and that it was a "wonderful co-incidence" that I looked so much like Louisa Ireland. I couldn't help wondering what Cilla would have thought about it.

Chapter 10

BUNTY ARMITAGE'S

COPY

CIRCUS GIRL SCRIPT – SCENES 62-68
SCENE 62. EXT. ROUGH TRACK
THROUGH THICK FOREST. EARLY
MORNING.
Several NOONGAH *hunters, dressed in mixture of European clothes and possum skins, and carrying spears, move swiftly and quietly through the bush. A light mist rises from the ground.*
(NOONGAH p.o.v.) *A caravan of horses and wagons winds slowly through the trees. At the head is a covered wagon, pulled by two horses. A woman holding a small child is seated beside the driver. Several children are peering from the back of the wagon, laughing and talking to the youth who is driving the following wagon. This wagon is pulled by six horses and is heavily laden with the canvas and poles for the circus tent. Following are three children and a*

youth, all mounted on horseback. Each leads a string of 3 or 4 horses and ponies.
The quiet of the bush is broken by the laughter of the children and the sounds of magpies and other birds.
(LOUISA's p.o.v.) Trees and undergrowth sliding past in front of her eyes. Sudden awareness of black figures sliding between trees. The image blurs. Close-up of LOUISA's face, startled, then curious.

ON THE WOODS POINT ROAD.

Close-up *of* NOONGAHS *chatting amongst themselves, gesticulating while huge grins appear on their faces.*

LOUISA *(pointing):* Artie! Did you see ...?

As ARTIE *turns to follow the direction of* LOUISA's *finger, the dark figures disappear in the morning mist.*

ARTIE: What?

LOUISA: Oh, er, I think I saw a – um – an emu.

ARTIE: Where? Quick, Perry, where's the gun?

LOUISA *(horrified):* No, no, you're too late – it's gone.

MICKEY: Blast! We could have done with some fresh tucker. Nothin' like a bit of emu stew. Gettin' a bit fed up with damper and bully beef.

LOUISA *heaves a sigh of relief. Caravan continues on through the bush.*

SCENE 63. EXT. ROUGH-HEWN PADDOCK SURROUNDED BY TREES. IN DISTANCE IS A SMALL EUROPEAN DWELLING. IN FOREGROUND A HALF-ERECTED CIRCUS TENT. DAY.

All the IRELAND *family are seen working at erecting the tent. Much activity, carrying poles, tying ropes, driving pegs, etc.*

SQUATTER *gallops into frame, halting in swirl of dust in front of* MR IRELAND.

MR IRELAND: G'day to you, sir. Much obliged for the use of your paddock.

SQUATTER: Glad to be of assistance. Must say, a bit of a novelty, having a circus in the front yard. Still, I guess the folk from Mullyup won't mind the trip out here for the chance at a bit of entertainment. Don't get much of that in these parts.

MR IRELAND: What about the dairy farmers? D' you think they'll come in for the performance?

SQUATTER: Oh, bound to. These cow cockies love a bit of a show – should pack the place out. Demned if I ain't as excited as the youngsters.

SQUATTER *turns his horse to ride away.*

MR IRELAND: Don't forget, now, the show starts at 8 o'clock sharp.

SQUATTER *rides off, waving his hat in farewell.*

SCENE 64.   EXT. CIRCUS TENT. EVENING.

A queue of ill-assorted men, women and children snakes away from the covered wagon, parked at front of tent, where MRS IRELAND *sits selling tickets from an improvised counter.*

Children run around excitedly, bunting waves from the guy ropes, a festive atmosphere prevails. MR IRELAND, *dressed in Victorian-style ringmaster's outfit, stands at front entrance of tent, yelling through old-fashioned megaphone.*

MR IRELAND: Come along now, don't delay. Step right up, Ladeez and Gentlemen, right this way for the Sensation of the Century. Direct from entertaining the crowned heads of the South Pacific, that's right, direct from a Royal Command Performance for Prince Tui Latui of Her Majesty's Dominion of New Zealand. Never before seen in the Wild West of Australia. Ladeez and Gentlemen, for your entertainment and delectation the one and only IRELAND'S CIRCUS!

SCENE 65: EXT. REAR OF CIRCUS TENT. EVENING.

Horses and performers in costume mill around the back entrance to the tent. ALFIE *leads horse with pad on back to where* LOUISA *is warming up with bending and stretching.* ALFIE *halts the horse beside her and makes a stirrup with his hands to help her mount.*

LOUISA *(blushing and slightly embarrassed):* Thanks, Alfie. You've really been a great help to us all since the storm.

ALFIE: You know I'd do anything for you Lu, er, Louisa, er for the family, that is. I'm more'n glad I got the chance to come and work with you. I don't know how long I could have stuck with those cousins of mine. I guess I really didn't want to be a dairy farmer. I can't imagine gettin' up at the crack a' dawn every day to milk plurry cows.

LOUISA *(laughing):* But you get up at the crack of dawn with us, anyway.

ALFIE: Yeah, but it's different, somehow. I mean, you all get up at sparrer's fart, oh, excuse my language *(shot of* LOUISA *trying not to grin)* and everybody bogs in, even your ma. And the littlies, too. *(Suddenly shy)* You know, Lu, I feel like I've got a family again.

LOUISA *reaches down to touch* ALFIE's *arm as he turns to lead the horse through the rear entrance of the tent.*

SCENE 66. INT. CIRCUS TENT.
LOUISA *enters ring through artistes' entrance, standing on pad on horse's back. Shots of* LOUISA *dancing on horseback alternate with shots of audience. There is no seating in the tent. People stand around the*

ring-fence, children in front, some children sit on the shoulders of men and older boys. A few women and children perch on bales of hay. The circus band thumps away next to the artistes' entrance. Audience is enthralled, laughing, cheering and clapping. The ring is lit by lanterns hanging from the king pole and quarter poles.

LOUISA's p.o.v. *Faces in audience rushing past in a circular blur.*

Cut between audience, LOUISA *and* LOUISA's p.o.v.

SCENE 67. EXT. CIRCUS TENT. EVENING.

Group of NOONGAH *children of various ages pushing and shoving, laughing and giggling as they peer through a gap in the canvas.*

(NOONGAH's p.o.v.) *Between the audience's shoulders and heads can be glimpsed flashes of* LOUISA *and horse as they circle the ring, echoing the* p.o.v. *of the* NOONGAHS *in Scene 62.*

MR IRELAND *appears suddenly behind the children. They scream in fear and delight and run away.*

MR IRELAND *(removing his hat and mopping his brow):* Silly little beggars. I was going let them in for nothing, too. Still, don't blame 'em for bein' afraid a' me. Can't imagine what they must think of us.

Camera pulls back and up from MR IRELAND, *gradually revealing the whole scene: circus tent glowing from within, continual movement of performers and horses around circus tent, wagon and living tents, encircled by the dark mystery of the forest.*
The sound of the circus band drifts faintly over all.

FADE TO BLACK.

Chapter 11

The day of the Really Weird Thing started just like all the other days we'd had during the shoot.

Getting up at dawn, at "sparrow's fart" as Alfie says in the script, had become second nature to me. Well, sort of. I had breakfast with the cast and crew, like we always do. Boy, the food here is just to die for. Don't know what I'll do when I have to go home and face young Beryl (that's my mum) and her pathetic attempts at cooking. Anyway, after the morning feed it was into wardrobe and make-up, as per usual.

The scene we were to shoot involved a long sequence with Louisa on the solo trapeze. I had to wear *that* costume, and although I still didn't like the leotard any better, I must admit I was looking forward to being a "real" aerialist after all the hard practising I'd done. (Oh, Kitty says that in the old days circus people always spoke of people practising, and of animals being trained.)

We were still filming near Meekatharra, and it was still boiling hot. When the summer comes we are going south to the forest country and down to Albany where the weather is much cooler. Won't have to worry about the heat then, just frostbite. The Irelands travelled from Albany, through the centre of Western Australia, via Perth, and ended up in Broome. Right at the moment we're in the middle bit of the story and the middle bit of W.A., then we go up to Broome for a couple of months in the winter (bliss, bliss, bliss), but end up in Albany. Talk about doing things back to front.

So, anyway, there I was in wardrobe, doing battle with the (new) fleshings and the blue and red leotard, talking away to Mrs Blainey. Or should I say, she was talking at me. I felt like doing what Cilla does when she doesn't want to listen any more. My best friend stretches one of her elegant, long arms to the side, flexes her fingers upwards, and says in a totally bored voice, 'Talk to the hand, the brain's had enough!' I tell you what, that chick is so-o-o cool.

'There, pet,' Mrs B droned on in my ear, 'so once you've done this scene, you've only got to wear this leotard two more times.' She lovingly stroked the faded velvet, sighing as she hooked the lacings tight around the back of my waist.

'Ouch! Come off it, Mrs B. I can't breathe.'

'Sorry, love, there, you do look splendid, every inch the little trapeze artiste.' Mrs Blainey stepped back to admire her handiwork.

As the wardrobe lady moved away from me, only a step or two, I had the distinct impression that she was fading from sight. I blinked, rapidly, then had to squint, hard, to bring her back into focus. I sat abruptly on a chair. I could feel the sweat begin to trickle down my face. Oh, no. Not again. Just like the first time I tried on this costume. What was going on? Was I ill? My heart thumped and I had to lower my head between my knees.

At last the pounding in my chest slowed. I strained to see clearly around the dim caravan. The racks of costumes that lined the van seemed to have vanished and I couldn't see Mrs Blainey, either. The lamplight was too dull. When I stood up, my head banged against a lantern hanging from the top of the covered wagon.

Wagon? Lantern? I sat down again and felt the hot sweat dry to icy fear on my skin. I must be really ill. I'd never hallucinated before. Was it the *boeuf en croute* we had for dinner last night, or the strawberries and goat's milk yoghurt I'd scoffed this morning before coming to wardrobe? I knew I shouldn't have given in to greed. And now I was dying, was already dead. Must be. How else could I explain whatever was happening?

'Mrs B? Mrs B? Mrs Blainey?'

Where was she? Suddenly I missed her endless chatter. Cautiously I stood in the confined space. It really was a covered wagon. Maybe I'd been sleepwalking (so what happened to the day that had just started?) and had woken in one of the mock-up wagons that were being used for some of the scenes. Even as I thought this I knew it couldn't be. None of those wagons smelt like this one.

Smell?

There were smells here that I don't think I'd ever come across before. I started sniffing, all my senses focusing on my nose. I could smell humans, sweaty, strong, but not unpleasant. Underneath was a hint of some flowery thing, maybe lavender. A strong waft of horse caught my nose and then I picked out the rank smell of the lantern. I wondered what was burning in it. Oil? Mutton fat? Who knows. Something strange. I sniffed some more. The canvas top of the wagon gave out a musty smell, a mildewy tang that reminded me faintly of the beach. And still there was something, something I couldn't put a name to.

'Louisa! Lu?'

My thoughts (and sniffs) were shattered by a boy's voice. I stood in the middle of the wagon like an absolute idiot. Sometimes my mind is like a steel trap. Sometimes it's not. The canvas at the end of the wagon was suddenly brushed aside and a head was thrust in.

'Come on, Lu, your pa's gettin' impatient. Interval's almost over and you should be in the ring-door waitin' for your cue.'

I peered at the speaker. A few years older than me, he had bright red floppy hair and one of those faces that people in books refer to as "open". He looked nice, kind of handsome, really, but he also looked worried and a little angry. I just stood and gaped at him. He reached through the doorway and slapped my ankle. I looked down in surprise at his freckly hand and arm. I looked in surprise at my leg. It was covered in fleshings, those fleshings. I looked at my body. I was still dressed in the blue and red leotard, but even in the dim light of the lantern I could see the fabric was new and bright, the colours sharp and the sequins sparkling.

'Come on, Lu. Come on. You know what your pa's like when he's anxious.'

He turned away from me. I jumped from the wagon and followed.

Chapter 12

The red-headed boy walked away from me in the twilight gloom. Like a sleep-walker I followed through the muddy field. I stepped carefully between the guy ropes and the mob of children and people rushing around leading horses and ponies to and from the circus tent.

The tent glowed in the gathering dark and I could hear excited voices raised within, a kind of swelling murmur like the ocean on the turn of the tide. The boy, young man, really, kept talking at me over his shoulder as we hurried along, but I couldn't make out what he was saying. Numb with disbelief, confusion, and goodness knows what, I continued to follow like a zombie.

It occurred to me again that I must be ill. Anything else didn't bear thinking about, but as I gazed wide-eyed at my surroundings I had the horrible suspicion that I had never been anywhere as real as this circus lot. The sounds, the smells, the squelch of the mud as we slopped along, the steaming pile of horse manure, these things were too solid, too definite, to be anything but real.

A large man suddenly materialised from the gloom and started growling at me in a kind of whispered shout. 'Come on, Louisa. Crowd's all back in, can't keep 'em waiting any longer. What have you been up to, girl?' He shot a fierce look at my companion who squirmed and kicked at the mud with his boot. 'Come along.'

The man, dressed in a ringmaster's outfit, grabbed me by the elbow and hauled me into the back door of the tent, muttering all the time about ungrateful children with no sense of responsibility. He stationed me behind the ring curtain and then, with a twirl of his vast moustache, vanished into the interior of the tent. The band gave out a brassy flourish. Drum roll. Silence. Then the deep, rumbling sounds of the ringmaster's voice boomed into the hush.

The red-haired boy appeared at my side. 'It's all right, Lu. You know his bark's worse 'n his bite.' He leaned forward and tucked a flower into the front of my leotard and then, hesitantly, brushed my cheek with his lips. He disappeared behind me and, to my horror, I realised what the ringmaster had been busy announcing. I tuned in to hear him say, '... yes, Ladeez and Gentlemen, for the first time in Western Australia, making her debut on the solo trapeze, direct from performing before the crowned heads of Her Majesty's Dominion of New Zealand – Miss Louisa!'

Again I felt the blood pound in my head. I began to sweat and everything around me blurred and rushed away. The music swirled in my ears, I saw the lights of the circus tent spin crazily around and I felt myself falling ...

'LouisaLuLuBuBunty ... Bunty ... Come on, wake up! Come on girl, here we go, you'll be right in a moment.'

I opened my eyes. Mrs B was bending over me, wiping my face with a damp cloth. Cherry was hovering at her side, a make-up brush held in her hand as she flapped and squawked around us.

'Mind her make-up. Gawd, I spent hours on her hair ... watch what you're doing.'

'What's going on?' The Boss hustled his way to my side. Together he and Mrs B helped me up from the floor and led me to a couch. 'Easy now ....'

'Just give her a bit of space, that's what I always say, needs a bit of fresh air no doubt, it's awfully stuffy in here.' Mrs B prattled on, fanning at my face with a piece of paper, concern written all over her face. 'Probably tied her corset too tight, poor love, sorry about that. Would you like a drink of water?'

While Mrs B wandered off on her mission, The Boss sat down beside me and took my hand.

'Bunty, are you all right? I know we've been pushing the schedule a bit these last few days. But you know what it's like. If we're here too much longer we could get caught in Broome in the Wet, and you can guess what a disaster that'd be.'

I nodded, and smiled weakly. 'I, er, I don't think this is anything to do with the schedule. I, er ....'

My voice trailed off. I mean, what could I say? Oh, excuse me, Boss, I think I've just indulged in a wee bit of time travelling? I don't think so. I could try: Sorry Boss, must have smoked some funny stuff and had a bad trip, what a bummer. Nah! Didn't sound like me. Maybe I should just keep my mouth shut and let them think whatever they liked.

'We'd better make sure you get enough to eat and proper bed times, young lady.'

'Get real, Boss, you're starting to sound like my dad.'

'Sorry.' The Boss chuckled. *'Faux pas* to the max.'

'Hey, where'd you learn to speak like that?'

'I'm not really old you know, only thirty three. Not exactly ready for the scrap heap. Yo dude!'

'Oh, yeah. Right.' Whatever.

Mrs B came back. 'Come on, drink this up, and then we'll get you out of that costume.'

The Boss went off, still muttering about 'rest' and 'food'. As if I didn't eat like a horse already.

'Mrs B, d' you know anything about this costume? Didn't you say it really belonged to Louisa Ireland?'

I gazed over my shoulder as the wardrobe mistress began to unlace the back of the leotard. My hand strayed to my throat in one of those unconscious movements we make all the time. My fingers brushed on something cool and fleshy. I looked down at my chest. A small white flower was tucked into the top of the costume. It was wilting in the heat of the van. A strong perfume rose from it as I plucked it out and held it to my nose.

In the mirror, my reflection gazed back at me. My face looked different. I remembered the feel of the redheaded boy's lips on my cheek. Had I really been there, on Ireland's Circus? In your dreams, girl, in your dreams.

Chapter 13

'Come on Perry, Artie, pull that harmonium a bit nearer. That's it. If you get it close to the door of the wagon I can just roll the canvas up a bit, give us a hand here, luv, and then,' Mrs Ireland grunted as she lifted the heavy fabric, 'and then I can pull up me stool, and off we go.'

Mrs Ireland sat down at the old harmonium and began thumping at the tune, "Jerusalem".

It was Sunday morning.

The circus was camped on the banks of the Blackwood River. Ahead of the family lay the towns of Nannup, Collie, Bunbury, and the long road to Perth. Behind the travellers lay hard weeks of slogging through mud and unmade roads to entertain the farmers and squatters, the timber-cutters and the small town dwellers of the forest country.

As the uncertain notes of Mrs Ireland's harmonium rang out through the chilly air, the little camp sprang into life. Perry and Artie vaulted over the harmonium and landed on the soft ground with a light thump. Mrs Ireland gave a startled squeak, but didn't miss a note. She waggled her head in affectionate bemusement.

Up from the creek ran Mickey and Winnie. They each led a horse. Water streamed from the animals' mouths as they finished their morning drink on the run. The pale sunlight shone on the horses' glistening flanks and mud flicked up under their hooves. Mickey and Winnie laughed as they saw their big brothers fly over the top of their mother's head. Quickly they tied the horses to tethering ropes and then the two youngsters ran to join the rest of the family at morning prayers.

'How great thou art, how gre-a-t thou a-r-t!'

As the last notes of the hymn died away, Mickey turned to his big brother Artie with a flourish. 'Thou sure art great, Art.'

Everybody had heard the joke before, but the younger members of the family collapsed in a heap of giggles. Mr Ireland glared them into silence.

'If we had a lion I reckon Pa could tame him with one of his looks,' whispered Queenie. 'He wouldn't even need a whip.'

After the open-air church service, the family scattered over the camping ground to finish their morning chores. The livestock had all been fed and watered before the weekly prayer meeting had begun, but the animals still needed to be groomed and there was, as usual, plenty of horse manure to rake into a neat pile. Mr Ireland had often been heard to boast *that 'Any circus lot* Ireland's *stands on is cleaner when we leave than it was before we got there'.*

'Louisa, Winnie!' Mrs Ireland's voice rang out over the small encampment. 'Come and peel the spuds. Queenie, you take those little ones for a walk, but don't go near that river, mind.'

The large Ireland brood, independent and self-reliant from an early age, for the most part cheerfully joined in the many jobs required to keep a small circus on the road – even if that job involved baby-sitting the youngest members of the family.

'Hey, Queenie. Why don't you help Ma with the spuds, and I'll take the kids for a walk?' Louisa startled herself. She usually did as she was asked, but was even more startled when Queenie replied, 'All right. But I get to lick out the custard bowl after we make the Sunday pudding.'

Louisa gathered Dandy, Leo and Ria around her and, singing a nursery rhyme together, they strolled into the surrounding bush. Bird song hung on the morning air, the sharp tang of eucalyptus filled the children's noses, and bush flies lazily buzzed in the late winter sunshine. Louisa breathed a deep sigh of happiness. The children gathered stones and feathers as they walked and she helped them identify the treasures they found.

In a relaxed and playful mood the little group strolled into a small gully filled with paper-bark trees and swamp plants.

'I wonder if the Garden of Eden was as beautiful as this', Louisa thought, her mind still filled with the sounds of the family hymn-singing. She stooped to pick a tiny spray of early-flowering boronia and held it to her nose. Louisa breathed deeply and smiled, inhaling the sweet, sweet perfume that rose from the drab little brown and yellow bell-shaped flowers.

'Come on, kids. It must be time for dinner, let's go back.'

'Aw, Sissy, d' we have to?'

'Not hungwy, Leo not hungwy.'

'Ria hungry, Ria hungry.' Baby Ria, only two years old, turned and ran down the ill-defined path. She disappeared into the bush before Louisa could gather her wits.

'Ria, Ria.' Louisa plunged into the bush after her. Leo and Dandy streamed along in her wake, yelling, 'Wait for us, wait for us.'

Louisa panted around a corner and there, on the other side of a large paper-bark tree, stood little Ria. At her feet curled a large black snake, motionless in the winter sunshine.

Instinctively Louisa thrust out her arms to stop Leo and Dandy from running past. Surprised, the two little boys gasped, and raised stricken faces to their big sister. 'Hush,' she mouthed at them. 'Don't move.'

Ria appeared oblivious to the arrival of Louisa and the boys. Some instinct kept her silent and still. Louisa felt her heart pounding in her ears. The snake lay drowsing, but Louisa was well aware of how dangerous a snake could be at this time of year. As the late winter days warm and grow longer, snakes are lured from hibernation by the promise of spring. Newly awakened snakes, eager to breed and to defend their territory, are aggressive and full of venom brewed through the long cold of winter.

Louisa felt reality stretch out in an infinity of directions. She knew she had to move, and move quickly, but through some quirk of perception she could clearly see what had to be done to rescue her sister, and she watched herself do it, all in slow-motion.

This wasn't the stuff of nightmares where your feet become bogged in clay and you can only move with great difficulty. On the contrary, Louisa moved with the quickness of light through a world suddenly slowed down to the space between two breaths.

Just as Ria opened her mouth to scream her terror, the snake uncoiled itself and headed for the child. Louisa, in one swift movement, snatched Ria into the air and jumped onto the striking snake, pinning its long body to the ground.

Now Ria began to scream in earnest. Louisa looked down at the shiny black snake as it thrashed between her booted feet. How she longed to scream too. Her strong arms held the little girl high above the frenzied snake, and sweat began to soak her clothes. Her arms trembled and her knees felt weak with fear and effort.

Dandy and Leo leaped up and down on the spot, crying, too distraught to be of use to the desperate girl.

'Get Papa. Go and get Papa!' Louisa managed to pant at the boys. 'Hurry.'

Ria's cries continued to fill the air.

'Come on, Baby, let's practice some tricks.'

Louisa knew she had to keep Ria's hysteria under control before the little one squirmed her way out of her big sister's arm. The baby's tears disappeared and she clapped her hands in glee.

'Hup,' she called. 'Hoopla! Balance, Ria balance.'

'Lu – what the heck ...?'

Louisa turned her head towards the welcome voice.

'Oh, Alfie.'

The young lad summed up the situation at a glance.

'Here, give me Ria.'

The snake, angrier than ever, writhed as it tried vainly to strike at Alfie as he moved nearer. He stationed himself well out of reach of the snake's deadly fangs and with legs spread, boots firmly placed on the ground, he nodded to Louisa and waited for her command. The long hours of practice that Alfie had done since he joined Ireland's Circus came to their assistance as he and Louisa slipped easily into their established acrobatic routine.

'When I call "three"', Louisa instructed the little girl, 'you jump into Alfie's arms. Ready. One, two ... !'

Louisa bounced Ria in her arms, once, twice, as she counted. On the call of "three" the delighted child flew through the air and landed in Alfie's steady grasp. He plonked her down on the ground next to her brothers, well out of harm's way, and then returned to face the demented snake.

'What are we gonna do, Alfie? I can't move.'

Alfie pulled a knife from his belt. Expertly he twirled the blade through the air and into the back of the snake's head, narrowly missing Louisa's boot. The snake's muscular body convulsed and its death throes threw the girl to the ground. Louisa rolled clear of the snake and watched in stunned relief as Alfie made sure it was dead.

The three children stood huddled on the far side of the paper-bark tree, their eyes wide with fear and amazement. Louisa lay still on the ground, panting, her mind a sudden blank. Alfie wiped the knife blade clean in the dirt and tucked it into his belt again as he stood and mopped his brow.

'Wow, Alfie, you're a hero.'

'Nah, Dandy, not me. Your big sister here, she's the hero.' Alfie stretched out his hand to Louisa and hauled her to her feet. 'Come on, Lu. You all right?'

'Yes, thanks Alfie.' Louisa felt the sweat dry on her body. Her knees were still weak but she couldn't help grinning at the look of concern on Alfie's freckly face.

'Alfie?'

'Yeah?'

'Ah, thanks – really.'

They stood grinning at each other like a couple of fools. Leo grabbed Louisa's hand and tugged at her impatiently.

'Let's go. I'm hungwy.'

'All right, come on you lot.'

Alfie picked Ria up, Louisa took Dandy and Leo by the hand and together the little band went marching back through the bush. Alfie sang at the top of his tuneless voice, "There was an old man named

Michael Finnegan" and the children laughed as they joined him in the nonsense words, all danger forgotten.

Louisa felt hot and exhausted and hungry. She also felt wildly happy, but she didn't quite know why.

Chapter 14

When we eventually got around to taping *that* trapeze scene, I understood, in a real way, some of the difficulties Louisa and her family must have faced on a day-to-day basis. Just managing their bulky costumes was hard enough. The simple fact that the girls had to wear fleshings under their heavy leotards, regardless of the heat, turned Louisa and her sisters into heroines, for my money. Not only were these old costumes difficult to move in, but they were also impossible to keep clean. I don't think drycleaners had hit the outback, then. Thank goodness for Mrs B, that's all I can say.

But, back to taping my first big circus scene.

After the usual costume and make-up dramas (and a *very* small breakfast) I found myself standing in the ring-door awaiting the cue for my entrance. I could hear The Boss yelling last minute instructions to the crew inside the tent and through a gap in the curtain I watched them run cables under the ring-boxes and carry cameras into position. The circus band was twiddling away just to the left of the artistes' entrance. Behind me, extras were shuffling around, waiting to take their places.

The Boss had decided he wanted to film the scene as one "take". This is quite unusual, Kitty told me, as normally each scene is shot in little disconnected pieces from different angles which are then edited together to give the appearance of some kind of reality. Evidently The Boss is known as an interesting director and for this scene he wanted to keep the cameras rolling and to move them around the action. 'I want a seamless flow, just keep the action moving and I'll see that we get the shots.'

Kitty thought this was an excellent idea. 'Boss, have you any idea how difficult it is for an aerial artist to repeat and repeat and repeat tricks for the camera? And you need to think about the heat. Bunty really won't want to stay up next to that canvas any longer than she absolutely needs to.'

I hugged Kitty in thanks. I'd been up on the trapeze for a rehearsal the day before and, let me tell you, it was hotter than hell. Heat rises, of course, and what with all the lights and stuff necessary for filming, it was an absolute furnace at the top of that little tent.

As I climbed higher on the rope ladder the super-heated air rushed into my lungs, taking my breath away and making me sweat like a pig.

The lights dimmed and Bonner Sergeant, the actor playing my screen father, came bustling through the ring-door curtain, scattering cast and crew in all directions. A chill went up my spine. My hair stood on end (sorry, Cherry). Bonner was wearing an old-fashioned ringmaster's coat and top hat. White britches covered his rather large bum and he had on highly polished, knee-high black riding boots, he carried a whip in one hand and with the other he twirled his moustaches. I'd never noticed before how much he looked like the real Mr Ireland.

Or did he? At least, he looked like the "real" Mr Ireland I'd seen in my "time-travelling dream", as I'd come to think of that peculiar episode. But, did Mr Ireland look like Bonner because I already knew the actor and had projected his image into my fantasy, or was something else really weird going on? I didn't have time to think about all that at the moment. It was getting far too complicated.

'You're on, Bunty.' The Boss materialised at my side, then disappeared with a casual, 'Chookers, kid'.

Kitty had told me (she was a fund of information) that this was an expression used mainly by dancers because wishing a performer "good luck" was considered to be bad luck. Figure that one out. Actors also say "break a leg", but for an acrobat that's not really a very cool thing to say, so chookers it is.

The band struck up a fanfare and Bonner Sergeant, as Mr Ireland, launched into his introductory speech. Before I knew it I was in the ring. Lanterns hung from the quarter poles and a chandelier, made from a cart wheel with large candles stuck all over it, hung from the centre of the tent and cast a flickering, yellow light over me, the band and the extras grouped around the ring fence. Blobs of melted wax fell in a little shower. I wondered how the horses would handle it.

My hands felt slimy with sweat and I hoped the riggers had remembered to attach a resin sock to the trapeze ropes. Powdered resin helps you stick to the trapeze. It's kept in a sock and attached to the ropes of the trapeze for convenience so you can puff it all over your hands and ankles and feet in a big cloud of dust. Reflected in the spot lights it looks really impressive and kind of romantic.

I walked into the ring with a light, skipping step, just the way Kitty had taught me. I stopped at the rope ladder which swung from the trapeze down to the sawdust at my feet. I grabbed hold of a rung with my left hand and with my right I made a "compliment", a stylised acknowledgement to the audience. Another piece of insider information from Kitty: circus performers never bow, they always hold themselves high, arms held up to face the audience with confidence and pride. The crowd of extras cheered and clapped. I loved it. I just loved it. This was real, for me. I knew I was acting, but it felt so right.

Surreptitiously I wiped my sweaty hands down the side of my leotard and then began the long climb up the swaying ladder. I could feel the heat from the candles but, as the trapeze was rigged off to the side of the chandelier, I didn't need to worry about having an unscheduled bikini wax. That's one fringe benefit I could do without – oops, sorry!

The trumpet fanfare of the band changed to a dreamy waltz tempo as I swung myself over to the trapeze, styled a compliment, and began the first series of tricks and poses that made up the opening to Louisa's aerial act. "Half angels", "bird's nests", back hangs, toe hangs – the tricks flowed into each other and with every turn and twist of my body I felt more at home.

The audience of extras, all dressed in period costumes, was cued by the assistant director to cheer and clap, but as I went through the detailed movements of the aerial routine I felt a change take place in their responses. The applause seemed more natural, more genuine. The audience was responding spontaneously, and I was really getting off on it all.

After my finishing trick, a swinging toe hang, I shinned down the ladder, complimented to the audience, right, left and centre, and flew through the ring-door. I was floating, high on adrenaline and a buzz of excitement.

I didn't need The Boss to tell me he was pleased with the "take", but when I heard him yell, 'It's a wrap!' I knew he loved it. And he didn't need to know that the whole time I was up there, suspended above the ring and the cheering audience, I was really somewhere else.

Chapter 15

DUCHESS FILMS
BUNTY ARMITAGE:
CIRCUS GIRL
SHOOTING SCRIPT

110. EXT. FORREST PLACE,

PERTH.   A   HUGE,

ARTIFICIAL   WATERFALL

AND LAKE CONSTRUCTED

FROM   WOODEN

SCAFFOLDING   AND

CANVAS   DOMINATES

MIDDLE   AND

FOREGROUND.   BEHIND

CAN BE GLIMPSED THE G.P.O. AND VARIOUS OTHER CITY BUILDINGS. DAY.

FX: General hum of city life. Voices, horse-drawn vehicles , cars, etc. Over-all sound of circus band.

Cam. 1 mounted on top of waterfall to show Mr Ireland.

Hold on Mr I as crowd mills around.

MR IRELAND, *dressed as an admiral, spruiks to the passing shoppers and office workers, drumming up a crowd. Behind him can be seen costumed figures on and around waterfall and lake.*

MR IRELAND (v.o.): Roll up, roll up, roll up! Don't miss this most Glorious,

Cam 3. Centre right. Shots of crowd with close-ups cut with general med. shots Carnival atmosphere.

Glamorous and Geographically Various and Versimilitudinous Romantic Rendition of the Famously Furious Escapade and Escape of a Modest Maid and her Eventual Evanescent Resuscitation and Rescue from Certain Death at the hands of Villainous and Vile Corsican Pirates, the Scourge of the Seven Seas. Stand aghast as the Maid is Precipitously Plunged into a Pit of Despair, a Pond of

Despond, a Place of Peril. Cheer and Give Thanks, Cheer and Give Money, as she is Selflessly Saved, Royally Rescued, by that Epitome of European Punctiliousness and Perfection, Salvador the Spanish Grandee!

In the middle distance, behind MR IRELAND, PERRY, ARTIE, MICKEY *and,* ALFIE , *dressed as pirates, clamber over rigging fixed to resemble*

Cam 2. Medium shot of pirates.

Cam mounted on ext. building on left of set. Intercut with shots from **Cam.1.** of Mr I and crowds.

masts of sailing ship. They perform handstands and head balances on rigging poles, and use the ropes as substitute trapezes.

QUEENIE, WINNIE and MRS IRELAND play brass, harmonium and drums off to left-hand side.

FX: Circus band dominates

Cam 2. Med shots of performers

Cut with **Cam 3.** shots of band.

LULU, dressed in Tyrolean style dirndl, leads a Dalmatian dog to centre front. Dog is harnessed and pulling a small cart filled with geese. As the geese leave the cart via a ramp, the pirates disappear behind rock situated right hand side of lake. Pirate heads peer over rock at LULU *and geese.*

LULU *leads the geese through a series of*

Cam 4. tracking Lulu and dog.

manoeuvres, then drives them into lake.

DANDY, LEO *and* RIA,

FX: geese honking, band playing

dressed in Tyrolean style, appear from left carrying bags of bread scraps to feed to the geese. They pass amongst the growing

Cam 3. Med shot of pirates

FX: 'melodrama' music from band.

Cam 1. Overhead

Cam 4. Tracking children through crowd.

Cam 3. Close-up pirate faces. Med shot as pirates move.

Cam 1. Overhead shots of chase.

FX: 'Melodrama' music.

Screams of Lulu and

crowd, selling the bags of bread.

Pirates move stealthily from behind rock, grab LULU, *and carry her away behind left of waterfall. Dog, geese and children chase after the Pirates.*

ALFIE, *dressed as a Spanish Grandee,*

appears at right of

children's shouts. Dog barking, geese honking.

Cam 4. Tracking Alfie.

Cam 1. Overhead of chase.

FX: Band plays 'chase' music. Shouts yells of Alfie and pirates.

Cam 4. Tracks up rigging

Cam 2. Continues tracking Alfie

Cam 4. Tracks pirates down and out

waterfall on pony. He rides through the lake and disappears in the direction of the Pirates, left.

Pirates appear right of waterfall and carry the struggling LULU to the top of the rigging where they lash her to a pole. They clamber back down the rigging and exit to left.

ALFIE reappears, right, dismounts from pony and climbs rigging on opposite side of lake to LULU. He

Cam 1. Overhead of Alfie.

Cam 3. & **Cam 4.** Track Alfie on wire

walks across tight rope, dancing and pirouetting, twirling cape, etc. until he reaches LULU.

He unties her, kisses her, and they slide down hanging rope to ground.

Cam 4. Cut between Alfie & **Cam 1.** on Lulu

Cam 1. Overhead of Alfie and Lulu.

Cam 4. Tracks Alfie and Lulu to ground, then follows pony from performance area.

They mount pony, ride triumphantly around lake, and exit left.

Entire cast re-enters from left and right to take a bow.

Cam 3. and **Cam 2.** Cut between performers and crowd.

Audience goes wild, cheering and throwing coins at the feet of the

FX: Band plays *performers.*

'chaser' music.

Crowd cheers,

applause, etc.

Sound of coins

falling on ground.

Fade.

Chapter 16

After all the strange things that had been happening, the last thing I needed was a visit from my air-head friend, Cilla; she can be such hard work at times. I was still trying to get my head around my "visit" to Ireland's Circus and I had only just got my breath, so to speak, after making my debut on the trapeze, when I heard her well-known squeal.

'Bunty!'

'Cilla!'

I ran out of my caravan, just in time to collide with her as she came around the corner. We grabbed hold of each other and jumped up and down, as excited as a couple of kids. Eventually we stopped long enough to stand back and size each other up. We held each other at arm's length. Cilla's long, blonde hair gleamed in the harsh sunlight. We both started to talk at once.

'You look gorgeous, girl. What are you doing here?'

'Look at you, Bunty, you're so tanned and just look at your muscles. I am impressed.'

We laughed. I flexed my biceps. Cilla squeezed one of my arms and we laughed again. It was good to have my friend back.

'Come on, I'll take you to the cantina. Would you believe, we have absolutely wicked coffee out here in the desert.'

'Yeh, right. Cappuccino Strip in Meekatharra. I'd like to see that.'

'It's true. The locals can't believe how we live out here. I've seen 'em down on the set gawping at us eating, for God's sake. Haven't they ever seen a body eat before? Fair enough, watching us film, but watching us eat!'

We sat with our coffees at a little table under a beach umbrella. I spooned sugar into my cappuccino and proceeded to eat the froth while Cilla stirred a sachet of sweetener into her long black. That points up the basic difference between us, I guess.

'So, what brings you up to Meeka? How'd you get out of school?'

'You won't believe it – I got this gorgeous, gorgeous, modelling contract.'

'Wicked. Where?'

'Broome.'

'Hey, unreal.'

'Sweet as. With this pearl company, or jeweller, or something. They just loved my hands, and my neck and my hair and, well, everything I suppose,' she said modestly. Well, modestly for Cilla. 'I get to wear all these unreal jools *and* get paid, *and* get to be the "face" of Pinkerton Pearls.'

'Yes, but,' I interrupted her, 'Meekatharra's nowhere near Broome.'

'No, but then the photographer for the Broome job got this other job and he figured I could do this other shoot for him as well. And the desert is the perfect place to do it.'

'Don't keep me in suspense any longer, Cill. Just what is this wonderful job?'

'Oh, just a little thing for the new *Excalibur*.'

Cilla gazed over my shoulder. I turned to see what she was looking at. It was a brand new, bright red *Excalibur* sports car.

'Wow!'

It was *so* Cilla.

The photographer (who was far too good-looking for anybody's health) took me for a burn out into the desert before he and Cilla took off for their shoot that afternoon. I think I left fingernail marks on the dashboard.

And, as much as I loved Cilla, I was glad I was not going where her life seemed to be taking her. What on earth was she thinking of?

I felt an ache in my heart after she left. We had only just healed our friendship, but if Cilla continued on this wild super-model path it seemed we could lose each other again. The pain only eased a bit when I thought about the red-haired boy and the "real" Ireland's Circus.

I wondered how I could get back there again.

Hi Girlfriend
Broome is wicked!
fith! and megga kool!
The modeling job is crual
and nect weekend I'm
going to the Broome Cup —
ther the Party Time!!!
love love love Cilla xx

Miss Bonti
Armitage
"Circus Girl"
c/o Post Office
Meekatharra
W A 6642

Girlfriend!	Miss Bunty Armitage,
ome is, like,	"Circus Girl"!
cked, filth &	c/o Post Office,
gacool! The	Meekatharra,
delling job is	WA, 6642
real and next	
ekend I'm going to	
Broome Cup – then	
Party, Party,	
ty!	
ve, Love, Love,	
la xxx	

Chapter 17

What's that saying? "Be careful what you wish for, you might just get it"? Pity I hadn't heard of it earlier.

The day after Cilla's visit we had to do some extra filming for the trapeze sequence. This meant I had to wear that costume again. I approached the dressing van with a squeezy feeling in my stomach. I wasn't worried about the trapeze now, I felt like an old hand, but I was worried about what might happen this time. What could happen? I mean, it was all just in my imagination, wasn't it?

Once again I stood before the mirror as Mrs B laced me into the leotard. Once again I watched my face change and blur as the darkness rushed in and I thought I would choke, or faint, or die. But this time I was prepared for it. This time, I whispered vaguely to my disappearing self, this time I'll find out what's going on.

I didn't faint. When I opened my eyes I found myself sitting on the back of a large, hairy horse. Warm sunshine beat down and animal smells wafted on a little breeze. I could hear butcherbirds singing and children's voices came sweetly through the surrounding scrub. I looked around. We could have been in Meekatharra still, but I wasn't sure. Red dust lay thick on the ground and swathes of everlasting flowers grew in bright carpets of colour beneath the stumpy trees. Spring.

The horse was tethered with a group of assorted horses and ponies. They cropped at the tough, yellowy grasses that grew between the flowers. I slid from the horse's back. He wore black and silver harness and white and black feathers poked up between his ears.

As I stood wondering, "what next?" a bunch of kids of various ages, all dressed in show costumes and leading a mob of Shetland ponies, came rushing up to me. Shouting and chattering they tethered and unharnessed the little fellows. Then in a swarm of good humour and laughter they trailed back the way they had come.

One of the departing boys turned and shouted at me, 'What's up wiv you, Lu? C'mon. You'll miss dinner if yer don't hurry.'

I waved vaguely at him, then turned, straight into the arms of the red-headed boy.

'Gotcha, Lu.'

'Ow!' I cried in surprise. I moved away from him but he grabbed my hand and swung me back to face him again. I was terrified he would realise I wasn't Louisa. I couldn't guess what would happen then.

'Lu, Louisa. Um, y' know – I, er ....' He put his arms around me. I gave him a shove and he staggered backwards.

'Oh. Oh, I'm sorry,' I blurted out.

He stared at me then. His ginger eyebrows knotted as a thoughtful expression crossed his face.

'Blimey, Lu, what's wrong? You look, I dunno, you look – different ....'

Panic spread from the pit of my stomach into the muscles of my face. No wonder he looked at me strangely. He thought he was looking at somebody he knew. I was looking at a stranger.

'Er, I'm not who you think I am.'

'Gee, Lu, what are you talking about? Are you sure you haven't got a touch of sun?'

'No, honestly – oh, dear ....'

I sat down abruptly on the hard earth and put my head in my hands. Well, I told myself, you asked for it and now you better work out how you're going to handle it.

'Look, whoever you are, I know you won't believe this, but I'm not Louisa. I'm Bunty, I'm from ....' I stopped.

The boy just stood and gawked at me as if I had two heads. Maybe I did. I stared back at him, my mind blank. We stayed like that for long moments, just staring at each other. I noticed after a while that he really was quite nice looking. He had soft green eyes and lightly tanned skin that seemed an odd but perfect match for his red gold hair. I kept thinking he was a boy, but he was probably closer to eighteen than to my own age. He had an unsophisticated look about him. He certainly didn't seem to be like any of the boys I knew at school. The longer I stared, the nicer-looking he got.

I don't know how long we stood like that, two statues stuck in the middle of the bush. I don't know how long we would have continued to stand there, staring, but at last he said, 'You're right, you're not Louisa. At least ... you look like her, I think, but ... this is – let me see your ear! Where's the mole on your left ear?'

I opened my mouth to reply, but before I could say a word the whole mob of Ireland kids returned through the scrub.

'Come on, you two. Youse'll be late for dinner, and you know how Ma hates us to be late.'

'Yeah, 'specially when she's spent all morning cooking.'

'Yeah, 'specially when she's made steamed pudding.'

'Steamed pudding,' chorused a trio of little kids.

'And we know what you two 'ave been up to out here in the scrub by yourselves.'

'Pa'll give you a leathering.'

'Yeah!' echoed the little kids.

The gang of bigs and littles clustered around us. The redheaded boy put his hands on his hips and glowered, unsuccessfully, at the group. They all laughed. Obviously they didn't think my new friend was really tough. I looked at his smiley green eyes. I didn't think he looked too tough, either. Just – nice.

The two littlest kids, a boy and a girl, took me by the hands and towed me along with the rest of the group. They gazed up trustingly at me and chattered away, non-stop, as we walked. They called me Lu and they called my companion Alfie.

I looked questioningly at Alfie over their dusty heads. He shrugged and turned away, his shoulders hunched in anger and confusion. None of the other kids took any particular notice of me as we trailed back to the circus camp but every time I turned to look at Alfie he flicked his eyes away quickly as if he had been studying me intently. The kids all chatted and horsed around in what I took to be their usual fashion, and once or twice the older boys made a sniggery remark about what Alfie and I had been up to while we were alone. As if.

I could see the canvas big top over the scrub and heard voices in the distance. Delicious cooking smells mixed in with the pong of animals and the waft of burning eucalyptus leaves from the campfire made my stomach growl with hunger. I inhaled deeply. I was terrified but I felt, somehow, more alive than I had ever felt before in my life.

A tall man, Mr Ireland I presumed, although he looked different in the daylight without his costume, appeared from behind the covered wagon as we straggled up to the fire.

'Heavens, Louisa, Alfie. Your ma's waiting to serve dinner. What the devil do you two think you're playing at?'

'Now, now, Percy, mind your language.' Mrs Ireland scowled at her husband, and then turned to scowl at Alfie and me. 'Hurry up, lass, get that costume off quick smart before we eat. I don't know what's come over you, you never were a dawdler before, and now just look at you.'

'Yes, Ma,' I said as if I'd called her that all my life.

Where should I go to get changed, in the wagon or in one of the small living tents grouped around the fire? What would happen when I took the costume off? Would the real Louisa suddenly appear? Would I find myself back in my dressing van on the film set? Aargh! Brain fatigue! I couldn't think any more.

I turned blindly from the group and some instinct led me towards one of the tents. Nobody said anything, so I figured I was on track.

Behind me I heard Mr Ireland say, 'I'm a bit worried about my Louisa.'

Mrs Ireland replied, 'Oh, it's just her age, Pa, just her age.'

The little tent was really something. Stained and patched on the outside, inside it was like one of the pioneer bedrooms you see in historic village recreations. It was better than anything we had on the film set.

Two narrow bush beds stood against the sides of the tent. The beds were covered in the whitest of white patchwork quilts and topped with pillowcases embroidered with delicate bush flowers. From the canvas at the head of each bed hung a fancy-worked and framed quotation from the Bible. In the narrow space between the beds was a beautifully carved chest covered with a lacy white cloth where a vase of everlasting daisies and a small, leather-bound Bible lay. The air in the tent was sweet and smelled of dried lavender.

This had to be Louisa's bedroom which she shared with one of her sisters. But where was Louisa? What was I doing here? There had to be some reason. There had been too many co-incidences and weird things happening for this to be just an accident. I had only one question in my mind: what next?

Chapter 18

I sat on one of the beds in the bright, white light. And leapt straight up again. Phew! No dirt on the quilt. I felt sticky and dusty and wondered how Louisa and her sister managed to keep their bedding so clean and white. Don't think I could. I looked around for some clothes to change into, then realised everything must be in the trunk. But, I thought, Louisa wouldn't put her dirty workaday clothes in there. So where? Under the bed – just like me.

I pulled out a flannel shirt and a pair of old jodhpurs, a pair of well-worn boots, socks and some weird-looking underwear that was covered in ribbons and tiny pearl buttons. Hastily I shoved the underwear back under the bed (I couldn't imagine wearing that) and pulled the other clothes on over the costume. I didn't dare take the leotard off just yet; the old costume seemed to be the key to everything.

Back at the campfire the family had started eating without me. I decided it was probably not a good idea to sit too near Alfie and I was afraid to get too close to Mr & Mrs or any of the older kids. So I found a place near the three littlest ones, balancing my bowl of stew on my knee and listening to their chatter. I had one ear on the little kids (who I soon worked out were called Dandy, Leo and Ria, just like in our film script), and one ear on what the others were saying.

The talk, at the "big" end, all seemed to be about horses and dogs and business to do with the day-to-day running of the circus. It was fascinating stuff, but I couldn't really concentrate on anything because Alfie kept sneaking sideways looks at me. I was too nervous to return his glance but I felt if anyone could help me, it was him.

Somehow I managed to get through the meal without giving myself away. The stew sat in the bottom of my stomach like a lump of lead and my head wouldn't stop whirling with unanswerable questions. I had an awful feeling as I helped pack up the dishes that I would have to do some household job, like washing dishes or peeling spuds, that would put me under the watchful eye of Mrs Ireland. I didn't think I would be able to fool her for too long at close quarters.

But I was saved from the chance of immediate discovery when Mrs Ireland told me to take the little kids for a walk as it was Queenie's turn to do the dishes. I grabbed the hands of the two tiniest kids and headed for the bush. Dandy scampered along behind us yelling, 'Hey, wait Lu. Blimey Charlie, wait for me.'

I could hear Mrs Ireland's voice in the background: 'Just watch your language, young man. I'll wash your mouth out ....'

Ria and Leo giggled and began chanting 'Blimey Charlie, blimey Charlie' until Dandy caught up with us and clipped Leo around the ear.

'You just watch your language, young man,' Dandy said in a good imitation of his mother's voice. Then it was my turn to laugh.

'Hey, Lu, can we play in the pirate's cave?'

'Please, please, please?' they all chorused.

'Where are we going to find a pirate's cave out here?' I wondered aloud.

'You know, Lu – where you go with Alfie.'

I didn't, of course, so what was I going to do? Then I had an idea. I would get them to lead me to the cave as part of a game.

'Okay,' I said. The three children looked at me as if I was speaking Chinese. I realised "okay" was probably a word they had never heard before. I would have to be careful about using slang.

'Okay-hokay-okay,' they chanted.

'Lu, you've gone mad,' Dandy told me. 'Perry's right, you've gone soft in the head over that Alfie. Hokay-okay.'

They all started chanting again, 'Oh, hokey-okey-hokey, oh, hokey-okey-hokey .....'

A light went on in my head. I began to sing, 'You put your left hand in, you put your left hand out ....'

They joined in, '... you put you left hand in, and you shake it all about. You do the hokey-cokey and you turn around, THAT'S WHAT IT'S ALL ABOUT, OH!'

'Oh!' I turned around, and bumped into Alfie. Again.

'Alfie – ah, pirates, um we're going to the pirate cave. Er, let's go.' I grabbed his arm and tried to pull him along.

'Whoa, Lu. Slow down. Pirate cave?'

'Yes, pirate cave, where – er – where we, er, where we go ... together. That's what the kids, the children, told me anyway.' I stopped, breathless. I couldn't look at Alfie. I scuffed awkwardly at the dirt with the toe of my boot.

Alfie glared at the three small children. 'Who's been telling tales?'

'Perry!' they yelled together.

'Why, that bloomin' tell-tale, I'll, I'll ....'

'Wash yer mouth out, wash yer mouth out Alfie.' Dandy, Leo and Ria were having a wonderful time, jumping up and down, yelling at Alfie and dancing round in circles.

I began to laugh and Alfie joined in, despite himself. It was a release of built-up tension for me, and probably for Alfie, too, but it was all just a game to the kids.

When the giggles died away I wiped my eyes on my sleeve and commanded in my best pirate voice, 'Arrh, me hearties, you gang of desperados, let's go.'

'Where?' Alfie asked.

'To the pirates' cave, of course.' I looked sideways at Alfie, embarrassed and suddenly shy.

Alfie blushed, and pushed ahead of us, yelling over his shoulder, 'Come on then, slow-coaches. What're you waitin' for?'

The cave was really only an overhang of rock on a scrubby hillside. The children screamed with delight and ran up and down, playing at pirates and getting horribly dirty in the process. I sat down in the shade of a straggly gum tree. Alfie perched on a rock beside me.

'I hope Mrs, er, Ma, isn't too angry about all these dirty clothes.'

'Why, Lu, now you sound more like your old self.' He peered at me closely as if he could read the truth in my face.

'Look, Alfie, I don't know how to say this, but I'm really not Louisa, you know.'

'Come on, Lu, stop playing games, stop kidding around. You're such a tease.' Alfie suddenly looked sad and worried. 'You're serious, aren't you? Sure you haven't got the typhoid fever or something? I'm frightened, Lu, I'm going to tell your ma...'

I reached out and touched him gently on his knee.

'Please, don't tell. I don't know what's going on, either.' I sighed. How could I explain to this sweet boy that I come from the Twentieth Century, that I'm involved in making a television series. How could I even begin to explain television, for heaven's sake. They'll think I've got more than typhoid fever, they might lock me up in a mental asylum.

Where to start? I cast my mind back to the script of "Circus Girl" in an effort to find a place where our different worlds might coincide, but the only thing I could come up with was the travelling magic lantern show. At one point in the script Ireland's Circus loses out on the chance to perform in an outback town because the picture show man had already got in ahead of them. The Boss explained to me that the magic lantern was like an early movie or DVD projector and the travelling picture show men with their novelty "moving pictures" were in direct competition with live shows such as the circus.

'Alfie,' I began, feeling like a complete idiot, 'have you ever seen one of those magic lantern shows?'

'Don't talk to me about those charlatans,' Alfie spluttered. 'Those sneaky, good for nothing mongrels go around stealing our audiences, as if things aren't hard enough as they are.'

'Okay, calm down. Um, obviously you're not going to like this, but that's what I do, that's the world I come from. We're making a story about Ireland's Circus for a magic lantern show, and I play the role of Louisa ...'

'Stop it Lu, stop joshing around. You girls are all the same, always playing jokes on us poor fellas.'

I grabbed his arm. 'No, Alfie, I wouldn't do that. I'm deadly serious. I come from the future. I know you couldn't possibly believe me, but in the film, the magic lantern story, I wear Louisa's leotard, you know, the trapeze one, and every time I put it on – I end up here. On Ireland's Circus. With you ....'

To my surprise, as I finally ground to a halt, Alfie took my hand and squeezed it.

'I believe you, Lu, or Bunty, or whoever you say you are. I do believe you. Dunno why. Maybe it's something to do with that funny word you keep using, "hokay" or whatever it is. Nobody 'round here uses words like that. Even so, I know you are really Louisa, I mean, y' have to be – wouldn't make no sense otherwise – but at the same time I can *feel* that you're not. Do y' know what I mean?

'Damn it all,' he went on, 'I've been really worried about Louisa, our Lu that is, these last few weeks. She's been acting really strange, disappearing for hours on end, not saying where she's been. And then the rest of the time she's like, I don't know, like a ghost, or as if she's not really here. Sorta vague ...' he leaned close and his voice rose in surprise. 'And you haven't got a mole on your left ear. Well, blow me down, that's gotta be some kind of proof, hasn't it?'

He continued to peer intently at me, our faces so close our noses almost touched. I took a deep breath and turned my head away. The longer I spent with Alfie the more attractive he became. I cleared my throat, gave a little nervous cough. 'So where is Louisa now? And why don't I see her when I'm here? Where does she go when I'm around? This is seriously weird, Alfie, and I don't know what we should do.'

'Tell Mr Ireland.'

'No!'

'Why ever not?'

'I – it just doesn't seem right. I think it would be best to wait, and – and see what happens. I wouldn't want Louisa to get into trouble, and if she did it would be my fault. We should try and find out more about what's going on, don't you think? Then we can decide what to do.'

'Yes, well right now I reckon we better get back to camp and do the evening chores. I'm bound to be in big trouble for skiving off all afternoon.'

We rounded up the children and headed back to the circus. Dusk was falling as we approached the camp and we could hear someone banging on the triangle to let us know that supper was ready. It smelled good. I followed Alfie and the children into the firelight.

Chapter 19

'Hey,' I called after him. 'Do you and Louisa really meet at the pirate cave?'

Alfie turned, a cheeky grin on his face. I didn't hear his reply. I walked towards him, my hand reaching out to catch him by the arm. I walked straight through him. I walked through the fire and the pot of stew. My outstretched hand banged into something hard. It was a mirror. I could see my reflection and behind me stood Mrs B, her mouth full of pins.

'There you go, pet, that should hold for this shoot, but mind you, after you've finished I'll have to do a bit of a repair. I swear you've put on more muscle since we began filming, not that you was skinny to start with.'

I rubbed my arm across my eyes. 'Um, Mrs B, what scene are we shooting?'

'Well, I don't know what's gotten into you lately, Bunty. Fainting and whatnot, and now you can't remember what scene. I just don't know. We're doing the cut-in shots of the trapeze sequence so really I suppose this'll be about the last time you'll have to wear this costume, I know you don't really like it but it is authentic, and I think it suits you a treat.'

While Mrs B paused for breath I tried to collect my thoughts about the coming scene. I didn't have time to think about where I'd been or what I had been doing there. The fact that I had spent practically a whole day with the Irelands and then returned to the costume van at *exactly* the same time that I had apparently left, well, that was just too much to think about.

I threw a quick "thank you" to Mrs B and ran out of the costume van into make-up. There I had another ear-bashing from Cherry and then I was on the set. Home again. It was all getting very confusing. I had a real home with my parents in the terminally boring suburbs of Perth, I'd found a natural home for myself, here, on the film set with all these wonderful, crazy actors and directors and crew, and now I had another home. A home in a past I could never really belong to, Ireland's Circus – and Alfie.

I have to admit, even though I had only seen this unlikely boy a few times, I was feeling something more than sisterly affection for him. He was definitely getting under my skin. Really, Bunty, I told myself, of all the dumb things to do, falling in love with a boy who probably died before your mother was born has to be the dumbest idea you've ever come up with.

'Over here, Bunty, just a few back-up shots and we'll be through for the day.' The no-nonsense voice of The Boss greeted me as I stepped through the ring curtain of the tent and into a pool of light. 'In fact,' The Boss continued, 'we're ahead of schedule and it looks like we'll be able to head out of here before the weekend.'

A chorus of cheers greeted The Boss's announcement. I think everybody was fairly savage about being in Meekatharra for so long. I know I certainly was and I couldn't wait to get to Broome.

I lay in my bed that night listening to the hum of the air-conditioner and thinking about Lulu's little camp bed and the way she had made a home in an old canvas tent. No two lives could be as far apart as Louisa's and mine, but somehow, for some reason, we were tangled up together. I wondered if I would ever meet her.

I had a dream that night that seemed as real as my other weird experiences. But I'm sure this was a dream. At least, I think it was a dream.

It was night, in my dream, but a full yellow moon hung low in the sky and I could see as clearly as in daylight. I was walking along a cliff edge. The sea raged below me and ahead of me walked a slim figure. This person (was it Alfie?) turned every so often and beckoned me on. The track on the cliff top ended. My companion took my hand and we floated out over the water.

The moonlight on the waves made a pathway to the cliff face. We followed the moon-path into a cave. The cave was pitch black but I could clearly see, lying on a pile of seaweed, the figure of a young girl. I looked closely. It was Louisa Ireland. One of her legs was twisted away from her body at a strange angle and her face looked pale and ill. The next instant I was back on the cliff top, standing next to a twisted, gnarly gum tree that grew through the middle of a large pile of rocks.

I was alone, my companion had gone. The wind began to howl and the branches of the tree banged against the rocks. The banging woke me up. It was morning and somebody was shouting and knocking on my caravan door.

'Wakey, wakey, rise and shine.'

'Erg, leave me alone.' I buried my head in the pillow. I was exhausted.

Dear Mum & Dad,
The country here is unbelievable.
The Boss & Kitty Warner are wicked
and so is the food.
We've only got one more week in
Meekatharra & then we're off to
Broome. Yay!
Hope the pooch is behaving itself!!
Lots of Luv, Bunty

Mr & Mrs Armitage
2 Swan Crescent
Outreach WA 6999

AIRMAIL

Dear Mum & Dad,
  The country up here is
unbelievable! The Boss and Kitty
Lambert are wicked and so is the
food.
  We've only got one more week
in Meeka and then we're off to
Broome. Yay!
Hope the Pooch is behaving
herself.
Lots of luv,
    Bunty

Mr & Mrs Armitage,
2 Swan Cres,
Outreach,
Perth,
WA

2 Swan Crescent
Outridge   Perth
Thurs 10th
Darling Bunty –

Lovely to get your card. The country up there certainly
beautiful. Your father and I have fond memories of travelling in th
area.

I'm so happy for you that everything seems to be going so well
you must realise what a big decision it was for us to allow you to g
off like this to film with all those people we didn't know, but Dami
Duchesne seems like an honest man. And, as it turns out, your Au
Jessie used to go to school with Kitty Lambert's brother (isn't th
just typical of Perth!) – so that makes me feel a lot happier about
all.

The Pooch sends her love, as do your father and, of course,
Your Loving Mum.

Chapter 20

CIRCUS GIRL SCRIPT – SCENES 472-475

SCENE 472. EXT. COUNTRY RACE COURSE. DAY.
In foreground *horses and jockeys dressed in racing silks are paraded around the ring. Crowd dressed in "Sunday best" mills around excitedly. In middle distance can be seen bookies and their clerks shouting the odds and surrounded by enthusiastic punters. A brass band can be heard over the top of it all.*

SCENE 473. EXT. LOOSE-BOX IN A COMPLEX OF SLAB-SIDED STABLES. RACE COURSE. DAY.
MR IRELAND *holds a racehorse by the bridle.* PERRY *and* ARTIE *dressed in racing silks are mounted on two horses which skitter around.* MR IRELAND *shouts instructions at* LOUISA *as she struggles to pull racing silks over her own clothes.* LOUISA *finishes dressing and tucks her long hair up under her racing cap.* MR IRELAND *gives her a leg-up into the saddle. The three horses prance around* MR

IRELAND *who continues to issue instructions.*

MR IRELAND: Now, don't forget – hold her nice and steady as you come round the bend. She'll want to go as soon as she sees the straight, but you've got to hold her in a bit. Just let her sit there – she'll stay behind *Sultan* nice and pretty, and then you can let her rip.

LOUISA: Yes, Pa. You've already told me.

MR IRELAND: Well, I'm telling you again.

ARTIE: But what if *Sultan* wants to go?

MR IRELAND: Look, son, *Sultan* hasn't got the breath for it. Soon as *Merriweather* gets a sniff of the winning post, she'll be off.

PERRY: But what about me? Y' know how *Lucky Legs* loves a gallop.

MR IRELAND *(tapping the side of his nose with his forefinger)*: Well, first and second place wouldn't be a bad day's work, now would it? And judging by the looks of some o' these nags, I reckon we've got a fair chance of bringing in third, too. *Sultan* isn't that short-winded. Ah, yes, the *Meekatharra Cup.* Now that is a prize worth winning. Imagine the publicity for the circus if we take off all three places. And a nice bit of cash, to boot.

LOUISA: But Pa, what if they find out I'm a girl?

MR IRELAND: Well, I'm not about to tell 'em. Are you?

LOUISA: I dunno, Pa. I've got a bad feeling about all this.

PERRY: Buck up, Lu, should be a good run.

ARTIE: You betcha, Lu. Let's go and show 'em, eh?

MR IRELAND: Remember Louisa, it's "just another show". Now, go on – and God bless you, lass.

SCENE 274. EXT. STARTING POST ON RACE COURSE. DAY.

Eleven horses and jockeys manoeuvre for position at the starting tape. Officials bustle around, yelling orders. The race starter hovers with pistol up-raised, ready to signal "off". LOUISA arrives late and pushes her mount through the milling horses just as the pistol fires. LOUISA is elbowed aside by a large jockey astride a very large horse. Her inexperience shows as she makes a late jump from the starting line.

(LOUISA's p.o.v.) *Merriweather's head bobbing up and down. Through the horse's ears LOUISA watches the other horses gather in a bunch under the control of their riders. Merriweather seems to be falling behind the pack.*

Long shot *of horses racing round the bend,* Merriweather *well to the rear.*

Medium shot *of* PERRY *and* ARTIE *neck and neck about three horses from the lead.*

Close-up *of* LOUISA, *intensely concentrating on the race, urging* Merriweather *on.*

Intercut *with shots of crowd, including* close-ups *of* MR IRELAND, ALFIE, MICKEY *and* WINNIE all urging LOUISA *on, but quietly.* WINNIE, QUEENIE *and* DANDY *are unable to control themselves and jump up and down, chanting and waving their arms in the air.*

Long shot *of horses entering the straight.*

Close-up *of* LOUISA *and* Merriweather *pulling out from the back of the field of horses and beginning to overtake, steadily and surely.*

LOUISA's p.o.v.) *Blur of horses and colours of silks as* LOUISA *and* Merriweather *move further up the pack. As they pass the large horse seen at the starting tape the rider strikes out with his whip, lashing* LOUISA *across the face.*

Medium shot *of* LOUISA *losing one of her reins and slipping forward over her horse's neck as she grapples to gather up the reins.*

Long shot *of* Merriweather *running to outside of track. The horse seems to be out of control.*

Cut to *shots of* IRELAND FAMILY *with anguished looks on their faces.*

Long shot *of* Merriweather *pulling ahead of the field as* LOUISA *pushes her on to the winning post.* Hold *on winning post as the rest of the horses stream across.* PERRY *and* ARTIE *fly past the winning post in second and third place.*

Close-up *of* LOUISA *as she rides to a halt.*

Medium shot *of* PERRY *and* ARTIE *reining in beside her, thumping her on the shoulders, shouting and cheering.*

Medium shot *of* IRELAND FAMILY *jumping up and down, screaming and cheering.* MR IRELAND *is waving a fistful of betting tickets in the air.*

MR IRELAND: She's done it – we've done it. Scooped the pool. Bloody beauty!

The IRELAND *children look at their father in amazement, shocked at his language.*

MR IRELAND, *too excited to worry about what the children are thinking, grabs* DANDY *by the hand and makes off to the winner's enclosure. The other children race along behind him. Everybody is talking at once. Nobody is listening, but they all have enormous grins on their faces.*

SCENE 475. EXT. WINNER'S ENCLOSURE. DAY.

LOUISA *and* Merriweather *are paraded around the ring.* MR IRELAND *steps forward and takes* Merriweather *by the headstall. In the background,* PERRY *and* ARTIE *walk their horses round.*

MR IRELAND: Well done, lass, well done.

LOUISA: Oh pa, we did it, we really did. And the boys ....

MR IRELAND: Wait till we tell your mother, eh? And the publicity, just think of the publicity.

MR IRELAND *is interrupted by the arrival of the* MAYOR OF MEEKATHARRA *bearing a large gold cup. He holds up his hand for silence from the crowd.*

MAYOR: Ladies and Gentlemen. It gives me great pleasure to present this prestigious prize to our plucky little champion here, er – *(aside to* MR IRELAND, What's his name again) – er, Master Lou Ireland who rode his brave little mare, *Merriweather*, to victory in front of his two brothers, Perry and Artie Ireland. *(The crowd erupts into cheers. The* MAYOR *raises his hand again for silence.)* This feat must be unique in the illustrious annals of racing in Meekatharra. Three cheers for the Ireland family.

The crowd raises three cheers as the MAYOR *hands the cup to* LOUISA *and shakes her hand. The* MAYOR *digs into his robes and produces a bag of money which he presents to* MR IRELAND. *They shake hands and* LOUISA *holds the Cup aloft. As she lifts the cup she knocks her jockey cap to the ground. Her long hair tumbles down around her shoulders.*

Close-up *of the* MAYOR's *shocked face.*

Medium shot *of shocked crowd. A muted roar rises from the now angry crowd.*

Medium shot *of* MR IRELAND *vaulting onto* Merriweather *behind* LOUISA.

MR IRELAND *(shouting)*: Perry, Alfie, get the kids.

Long shot *of* PERRY *and* ARTIE *leaping onto their horses. In the* foreground *are* MR IRELAND *and* LOUISA, *mounted on* Merriweather, *and the angry and bewildered* MAYOR.

MR IRELAND: Go, go, allez, allez!

LOUISA *rides her horse at the barrier around the winner's enclosure, scattering the crowd. The* Meekatharra Cup *is tucked awkwardly under her arm.* MR IRELAND *clings on desperately behind her.* Merriweather *clears the fence, closely followed by* PERRY *and* ARTIE *on their horses.*

Long shot *of* LOUISA, MR IRELAND, PERRY *and* ARTIE *riding flat-out down alley-way between stables. People scatter in all directions.*

Medium shot *of* WINNIE, QUEENIE *and* DANDY *standing outside stable.*

P.o.v. WINNIE, QUEENIE *and* DANDY *as horses and riders approach them.*

MICKEY *and* ALFIE *appear, running through the crowd.*

Medium shot *as* MR IRELAND *leaps from behind* LOUISA, *throws* WINNIE *onto another horse waiting in the stable, and vaults up behind* WINNIE.

 MICKEY *and* ALFIE *appear, running through the crowd.* MICKEY *and* ALFIE *leap onto another horse tethered nearby.*

Medium shot, PERRY *and* ARTIE *scoop* QUEENIE *and* DANDY *from the ground as they ride past.*

Medium shot *as the five horses and nine riders gallop through more stables and out into the open.*

Long shot *of horses and riders galloping through the racecourse gates pursued by mounted stewards, assorted mounted jockeys, officials and the angry crowd on foot. A few dogs join in the chase, barking and generally creating more havoc.*

Long shot *from above of the* IRELANDS *pulling further and further away from their pursuers.*

Medium shot *of group reining in, horses puffing and blowing, riders sweaty and panting. All have broad grins on their faces.*

Close up *as* LOUISA *holds the* Meekatharra Cup *over her head.*

PERRY: Three cheers for the Ireland Family Dare-devil Riders!

ARTIE: Hip-hip ...

ALL: ... Hooray!

MR IRELAND: And three cheers for Louisa and the bag of gold.

He brandishes money bag in the air. They all cheer, loudly and heartily.

Camera pulls back and up *they cheer and throw their hats in the air.*

FADE TO BLACK.

Chapter 21

'There you are pet, all ready to go.'

Mrs Blainey stepped back and looked over my shoulder at the two of us in the mirror. My reflection winked at her, and our wardrobe lady grinned back at me. I was dressed in the troublesome leotard again, but I felt fine, normal. Nothing seemed to be happening. Had my time-travelling come to an end?

'Thanks, Mrs B.' I turned round and gave her a peck on the cheek. Then I ran down the steps, out of the cool of the dressing-van and into the bright sun of another perfect day.

My feet had hardly touched the ground before I stopped and looked around, surprised once again by the suddenness of the transformation. Gone was the film set and in its place was Ireland's Circus, sweltering in the tropical sun. Gone was the flat dust of Meekatharra, and in its place was the brilliant blue of sea and sky, the lush green and purple of bougainvillea twined around palm trees, the red pindan dirt merging into yellow sand. This had to be Broome.

The circus tent looked shabbier than I remembered it, stained red and brown and patched in several places. Two wagons, a buggy and a couple of living tents clustered close to the side-walls of the big top and I could see the circus livestock corralled in make-shift yards at the rear of the lot. I walked around the tent towards the front door. Against the far side of the tent was a rambling building. A rough, hand-lettered sign proclaimed that this was the Continental Hotel. As I watched, groups of men wandered in and out of the hotel doors; some of them seemed to be drunk and some of them were singing, out of tune and loudly.

I didn't know what to do or where to go. I was still wearing the costume, but it obviously wasn't show time. The tent and the animals drowsed in the late afternoon sun. Apart from the voices of the drunks singing at the pub next door the lot was silent, asleep, waiting for the evening performance.

The sun was hot. I moved into the shade of the tent and stood chewing my lip, wondering what next. Alfie was next, of course. He seemed to be my point of reference and somehow connected me to this strange, other world. A loud, tuneless whistling told me that Alfie was headed my way. I stepped out of the shadow and into his path.

'Gee, Lu, you gave me a start. Louisa? It is you, isn't it?' Alfie peered at me uncertainly.

'No, Alfie, it's Bunty. I – I'm sorry.'

'Darn. I'm blowed if I know where that girl has got to again.' Alfie scowled at me, as if it was my fault. Maybe it was. 'Come on,' he muttered, 'you better get out of that costume before somebody starts asking awkward questions.' He grabbed my arm and dragged me towards one of the living tents.

'Alfie! This is your tent. D' you think this is wise?'

He didn't answer. I looked around. Rough, boyish, this tent was so different from Louisa's spotless bedroom. Bits of saddlery, pieces of leather, grooming brushes and clothes lay jumbled together on the little camp-bed.

Alfie grabbed up a shirt and a pair of trousers. 'Here, put these on. Er – over the costume.' He blushed and turned his head away. I smiled to myself, but did as he suggested. I looked at my feet, still clad in the leather acrobat's boots, and wiggled my toes.

'Boots, boots,' he said distractedly and dug underneath the bed. He hauled out a pair of gumboots. 'Bit big, I'm afraid ...'

'... but they'll do for now.' I finished his sentence. We looked at each other, and grinned. Whatever else was going on here I knew that Alfie and I really liked each other. There was some kind of – watcha call it – rapport, as if we had known each other before. Or, I suddenly thought, as if we knew each other in the future. As if we'd always known each other. Nah, ridiculous. I was getting confused again.

We stepped out of the tent. Alfie squinted off towards the west, over the low, scrubby sand hills that lay behind the tent and the pub.

'By crikey, don't like the look of that.'

I gazed where he pointed. I could see a bank of black clouds and as we watched the clouds flashed with sheets of lightning. The palm trees rattled their fronds in a sudden breeze. I felt cold, even though the day still steamed and sweated and the sun shone bright and hard.

'Mr Ireland is a stubborn old coot.' Alfie shook his head in exasperation 'The locals have warned him. The Wet, y' know.

They said we'd better stop showing. This time of year, cyclones are likely to come in at any old plurry time, but you can't tell him, he knows best. I don't like the looks of that, but.'

I didn't either, I have to admit. Alfie shook his head again, turned away from the looming clouds and headed towards the beach and the bright, turquoise bay. I tagged along, half running to keep up with his agitated stride, stumbling in my borrowed gumboots.

Chapter 22

By evening, and show-time, Louisa still hadn't returned. Somehow Alfie and I managed to cover up for her. We played a kind of chess game, moving carefully round the family, making sure I was never alone with Mr or Mrs Ireland, keeping my distance. I heard Mr Ireland complain to his wife that 'that demmed gel' seems to be 'off in dream-land again'. I spent as much time as I could grooming the horses and ponies. Boy, did their coats gleam in the ring that night.

It really is amazing how you can remain invisible if you keep moving (and thinking) fast enough. I had to dress in the tent Louisa shared with Winnie but as she was only about ten years old she didn't appear to notice anything strange. There was no reason why Winnie should imagine for one moment that her adored big sister wasn't who she seemed to be.

Earlier Alfie had told me the "running-order" of the show and what had to be done in between each item on the programme. I was sure I could do Louisa's trapeze act, the riding and even the tight-wire

– after all, these were the routines I had been practicing so hard for the past couple of months – but as show-time drew nearer I was packing it. I really didn't know how I would be able to fake all the other bits and pieces, like the tumbling act and the juggling – and playing in the band, and knowing what horses or ponies to fetch, and, and … the list seemed never-ending. I felt sick with worry, and that, in the end, is what saved the day.

Just before the performance began my poor stomach finally rebelled. Mr Ireland (embarrassingly) found me having a spew behind the horse yards and told me I'd best go and lie down for a few minutes but, he reminded me, 'Make sure you're back in time for the overture'. I felt too sick to do anything else, so I did as he ordered.

Mrs Ireland came into Louisa's tent, felt my forehead, and said I should take the night off. 'But, Louisa,' she said, 'I think you'll still have to do the trapeze. We can cover you for the other acts, and quite honestly you won't be missed in the band, but I don't think Winnie is quite ready to go in with her aerial act yet. Sick or not, you'll just have to do it. The audience won't take too kindly to missing out on a beautiful young lady on the trapeze.'

'All right, Ma,' I whispered.

I didn't have to do too much acting. I really did feel feverish and wondered how I was going to manage to carry this thing off. And why did I need to continue with this charade?

Partly it was because of Alfie.

We'd spent that afternoon walking on the beach, trying to make some sense of the whole mad situation. Although we were no nearer the truth we had come to a kind of truce; Alfie said he would believe me – for the moment. And we both felt we should say nothing until we could work out what was going on, but I think it was only because he loved Louisa that he agreed with my idea. I could see how much he cared for her and he wanted to protect her, from herself, from this situation, and from her father's unpredictable temper.

And, if the truth be known, I was a little in love with Alfie myself and I didn't want to make trouble for him. Stupid chick. I knew it was hopeless to feel like this, insane really, but you can't always help the way you feel, or who you feel it for. So I was willing to help Louisa and Alfie because I couldn't shake the idea that I'd been sent here for some purpose. Otherwise, where was the sense in it all?

So, what now? Here I was, sick and useless while the rest of the family rallied round and made emergency arrangements to replace me in some of the acts. I soon realised that if you were a member of Ireland's Circus you didn't get sick. That old cliché, "the show must go on" certainly seemed to be true, so I had to do my bit, even if it meant climbing out of my sickbed to do it. What an introduction to the real circus.

I lay in the tent while all around me I could hear the pre-show sounds of the circus lot. Beneath the noise of excited people buying tickets, the sounds of horses and dogs, the cry of Mr Ireland's 'roll up, roll up!' and the discordant notes of the band, I could hear an ominous roar. It was the wind. The black clouds on the horizon Alfie had pointed out to me earlier were now surging overhead, pushed and blown by the strengthening wind.

Through the flap of Louisa's tent I could see a full moon flitting and pulsing behind the gusting clouds. The locals were right; Mr Ireland should have cancelled the performance.

By the time the show started the wind was blowing hard. Mr Ireland and the boys raced around between acts, hammering in extra pegs to storm-guy the tent. I could hear them shouting above the noise of the approaching storm but before the interval break came the wind seemed to die down a bit.

Mr Ireland stuck his head in the flap of my tent and shouted, 'Come on, lass. Off that bed. We'll have time to finish before the storm really hits – can't send the public away dissatisfied with only half a show – not after they've paid good money. I want you in the ring-door in two minutes.' He disappeared back into the darkness.

Surprisingly, now that I really had to come up with the goods, I stopped feeling nervous. My mind cleared, my stomach stopped doing flip-flaps, and I realised that I was actually looking forward to performing. I made it to the ring-door right on time.

The wind had died away a bit but, as I loosened up and waited for the second half of the show to begin, I was very aware of how the big top jumped and shuddered with each gust. The lanterns that lit the interior of the tent with a warm, yellowish glow swung wildly and created strange, leaping shadows on the canvas walls. None of the Ireland's seemed particularly worried and before I had time to really think about the situation I heard Mr Ireland announcing Louisa's act. I guess it was my act, now.

'Ladeez and Gentlemen – for the first time in the Wild West of Australia, direct from a successful tour of Her Majesty's Dominion of New Zealand ... high above your head, on the solo trapeze ... Miss – Louisa – IRELAND!'

The band played a fanfare. I stood behind the ring curtain, my hands clutching the red velvet, frozen to the spot. Somebody shoved me in the back and into the ring. I blinked in the sudden light, and then noticed Alfie holding the rope ladder. In a trance I walked towards him and fumbled at the rungs. He winked at me and I grinned back and I felt strength and happiness flow through me. I could do this. I knew I could. This was what I had been practising for; this was the reality, my big test. I complimented to the audience, and began to climb.

I swung myself over to the trapeze, styled another compliment and began the first series of tricks and poses that made up the opening to the act. "Half-angels", "bird's nests", back hangs, toe hangs – the tricks flowed into each other and with every turn and twist of my body I felt more at home.

My mind went back to another day, a day of filming this very same act. I began to feel very confused. I couldn't remember where I was. Was this the film set, or was I on Ireland's? My thoughts whizzed round and round. I had to stop this, I had to concentrate. Dangerous, Bunty, this is dangerous. Concentrate.

Yesterday, today, tomorrow. They all seemed mixed up somehow, different, and yet the same.

Just when I thought I was really losing it the wind began to blow again. All the side-poles in the tent lifted up and smashed down with an almighty thump. The lanterns bounced and some of the lights went out. A couple of women in the audience screamed. I wanted to scream, too, but my mind was suddenly clear. I didn't want to end up on the ground – now I was focused.

The band kept playing, so I kept performing, working through my repertoire of tricks and poses. The audience settled back, reassured by the calmness of the circus folk and soon I was shinnying down the ladder and styling my final compliments in the sawdust ring. Alfie gave me a big grin and a thumbs-up as I skipped out through the ring-door, just like Kitty Lambert had taught me. She would have been proud of me. Over the thump of the band I could hear the storm, louder than ever.

At the back of the tent all was in chaos. People, dogs and horses ran in all directions. Overhead the sky boiled with lightning and thunder and huge black clouds raced across the full moon. Trees moaned as the wind increased and the tent began to flap alarmingly. I saw Mr Ireland leading a horse towards one of his sons. Lightning flashed and the horse reared in fright, then broke away and galloped off into the night. Mr Ireland shouted at the boy. I couldn't hear what he yelled, but the boy turned away in pursuit of the horse. Mr Ireland raced into the tent, beckoning for Alfie and the others to follow. The audience was streaming from the front of the tent which leaped and strained at the ropes like a wild beast. Heavy rain began to fall as I turned and ran back inside the big top. I could see the jagged lightning through the thin canvas. Light filled my eyes for a second, and then the world went black.

Chapter 23

Louisa was sure Merriweather had come down here, screaming with terror when the storm hit. There was too much rain, now, to see any hoof prints but she could feel it, inside. Instinct told her this, just as instinct had made the horse run blindly away from the lightning strikes and the falling trees.

Needles of rain beat at Louisa's skin and stung her eyelids. The wind howled and whipped the air away from her nostrils. She panted and coughed, unable to breathe as she pushed blindly through the scrub, through the sand hills, towards the sea. Overhead, low clouds scudded and raced across the full moon as lightning continued to flash and thunder to crack. The wind still blew but there was a change in the air, a promise that soon the storm would pass. Louisa was exhausted; she continued to search, the thought of the missing mare spurring her on.

Without warning the scrub gave way to rough sandstone. Louisa slithered to a halt as the treacherous ground became the crumbling edge of a cliff. The moon flickered through the clouds and cast its light on the pounding sea. Louisa felt sick and sat down abruptly. Then she lay on her stomach and peered fearfully over the edge.

The lightning continued to flash, but less frequently now, and the moon splashed light along the heaving waves. Louisa squinted into the rain, searching the rocks below for any sign of the missing animal. Merriweather was more than just her favourite horse; the mare was a highly-trained and valuable circus performer and shared a special bond with Louisa, the kind of trust that can only be built through long hours and days and years of training.

Louisa stood up cautiously on the brink of the cliff and called through cupped hands. Her voice was tiny, lost in the sound of roaring surf and wind. Her eyes felt hot with unshed tears, but she refused to give in, refused to believe her horse was gone. She tightened her fists into hard balls of determination and began to walk along the cliff top. Every few yards she stopped and called to the missing horse and she lay flat on the rough path again to scan the jagged shore below.

A small movement on the rocks caught her eye, a shadow moving on shadow and a faint cry drifted through the noise of the storm. Louisa peered through the rain. There! It moved again. Too small to be her horse. What was it? A child? She desperately focused on the small black bundle. Maybe it was a child, maybe it was just a baby seal caught on the rocks and stranded by the storm. Louisa leaned further over the cliff, eyes and ears straining.

There it was again, a faint crying, a baby's pitiful wailing. She watched as the shadow reached thin arms into the windy night and again she heard the almost-sound of sobbing above the storm. Louisa's heart contracted with fear and pity. She longed to go home, home to the safety of her family, but she knew that, much as she loved Merriweather and could not bear the thought of abandoning her search for the mare, her first duty must be to try to rescue the stranded baby.

She wasted no time in further thought but scoured the cliff-face for a path to the rocks below. As she searched, the clouds cleared from the western sky. The full moon hung heavy on the horizon and bright yellow light streamed across the ocean, lighting the cliff-top and casting deep black shadows around the rocks below. Louisa momentarily lost sight of the bundle on the rocks but she still seemed to hear its cries behind the sobbing of the wind.

A tree growing crookedly from a clump of rocks loomed in front of her. From the base of these rocks a faint path slithered over the edge of the cliff and disappeared into the moonlight. Cautiously, feeling her way step by inch by step, Louisa worked her way down the cliff. Shattered rock and pindan dust slid like silk beneath her boots and her nails broke and tore as she scrabbled to keep her balance on the treacherous path.

The wind still howled and beat at her ears and she strained to hear the baby's cries above the pounding sea. With a rush, in a flurry of sand, Louisa reached the end of the path. Her boots slid on seaweed and she clutched at a barnacle-covered rock to stop herself falling.

The shadows lay thick and impenetrable around the sea-smoothed rocks. Louisa tried to orientate herself. Where was the baby? She listened, and heard nothing but the ocean's roar. She looked, and saw nothing but fantastic rocks painted yellow by the moon and flanked by inky shadows. Seaweed lay in smelly heaps among the rocks and heaved and swelled as the waves gushed in and out.

Louisa realised what a fool she had been. Of course it wasn't a seal this far north, or a baby at all, only a heap of seaweed bobbing on the tide, buffeted by the wind. But the crying? She'd heard that, hadn't she? Fatigue and confusion clouded her mind. She gave a sob of frustration and anger at herself as she turned towards the narrow path to begin the climb back to the top.

She had only gone a few feet when she heard the crying again. She paused, thinking wildly, wondering what to do. Had she been mistaken? Was there, after all, a baby? She twisted her head stiffly over her shoulder, straining to locate the sound of the cry. Then she saw it. Not the baby. Not a seal. But a *huge wave, rising and growing from the black ocean, flecked with golden moonlight. Huge and growing bigger as she watched. Louisa held her breath and scrambled upwards, torn nails digging into dirt and rock. The wave rolled on, smashed against her legs, sucked at her body, drew her down ... down ... then flung her up, up. Then smashed her high against the cliff face.*

Chapter 24

When I think back on that crazy night of the storm I still can't work out what really went on. One minute I was running into the tent, the next minute I was out in the middle of the bush. The storm was still raging. Was it the same storm? I had no way of knowing. I didn't have a clue what was going on. I still don't.

But there I was, drenched. I was still wearing the costume only now it was wringing wet and weighed a tonne. My hair flapped and blew in my eyes and mouth, my ring boots were full of water and I slipped and slithered as I ran. Why was I running and where was I running to? I could hear somebody calling 'Louisa, Lu, Lu,' and realised it was me. A young man's voice called over and over, 'Louisa, Bunty, Louisa'. It was Alfie, and his voice came and went on the gusting wind.

I stopped running. I needed to think. Alfie loomed up beside me and grabbed my arm.

'Bunty, thank God you're all right.'

'What's going on? I'm scared, I don't know what the hell's going on.'

Alfie bellowed over the noise of the storm, 'We've got to find Louisa. Help me, Bunty, help me. *Merriweather* has gone, I saw her heading to the sand dunes. Louisa must have gone after her. She was here only a few moments ago....'

I didn't have time, then, to wonder how Alfie knew it was me he was talking to and not Louisa, but as I looked at his face, white with desperation and fear, I finally knew the reason I had come to Ireland's Circus. I squeezed his hand.

'It's okay, we'll find her.'

I turned away and leaned into the wind. I was a feather, I thought I would blow away but I knew I was headed in the right direction. Alfie staggered beside me and grabbed my hand. Together we struggled through the sand hills, heads bent, too breathless to speak.

Soon we came, as I knew we must, to the edge of a cliff. The moon broke through the clouds and I saw before me the image of my dream, the fat, yellow moon hanging low in the sky and casting a golden stairway upon the black and raging sea.

'Come on, Alfie, this way.'

I tugged at his sleeve and ran off along the cliff. A tree rose up out of the cliff top, a twisted, gnarly gum tree that grew through the middle of a large pile of rocks. I wasn't surprised to see it there. Alfie panted up behind me and I pointed to the barely visible path winding down the cliff face. I put my mouth to Alfie's ear and shouted at him, 'She's down there somewhere. I know she is.'

He grabbed my hands and pulled me close. 'I dunno what's going on, Bunty, but I'll always remember this.'

His lips brushed mine. My mouth felt numb with cold and rain and I felt the hot blood rush into my face. I turned from him and led the way down the cliff.

It's a miracle we weren't blown off the cliff face or washed to our deaths off the greasy rocks. Mounds of seaweed rose and fell as the waves smashed in and out over the rocky ledge we eventually landed on. I barely needed to look around to know where I was. Golden moonlight picked out another faint path leading up from the base of the cliff.

'There's a cave up there – she's in there, Louisa's up there. Let's go, we've got to get her before the tide comes in.'

Alfie looked at me as if I was mad, but he followed me anyway. I could hardly breathe by now; I was so exhausted I could barely put one foot in front of another. The wind still blew but the rain was easing off. The lightning, too, seemed to have stopped. And still we climbed, over rocks, around rocks until, suddenly, a large black shadow on the cliff wall became a cave.

'In here.'

We moved into the shadow. The moonlight followed and there, lying on a pile of seaweed, just like in my dream, was the missing Louisa, her left leg twisted away from her body at a strange angle. I shuddered with sudden cold. Now I was really frightened.

Alfie gave a cry and fell to his knees. He grabbed Louisa's pale, limp hands and rubbed them roughly as if to bring some warmth to them, then he kissed her on the eyes, on the lips. My eyes filled with tears. I was a ghost, not noticed here.

'Er, Alfie,' I coughed to get his attention. 'Time for that later. We've got to get her out, now – the tide ... it's a king tide ....'

'Maybe we should go for help – Mr Ireland ....'

'No, *now*. We must take Louisa with us, *now*.'

My voice sounded harsh in my ears and Alfie's head snapped up. He stared at me for a long second, then jumped to his feet as my voice whipped him into action.

'If you carry her under the arms, I can manage her feet. Just be careful of her leg. Wait a minute, give me your jacket, Alfie.' I folded the damp coat and hurriedly improvised a bandage around the injured limb. 'Okay now, easy does it.'

We manoeuvred Louisa into position and carefully picked her up. Her face was dead white in the moonlight and she groaned faintly as we lifted her. Alfie backed out of the cave onto the narrow path.

'Careful!' I snapped, unnecessarily.

'This – this isn't very practical.' Alfie grunted as his heel hit a rock and he staggered a bit. 'I can't see where I'm going. Maybe I should carry her over my shoulder.'

Poor Louisa. Poor Alfie. We managed to get her over Alfie's shoulder and slowly, with a lot of shuffling around as we negotiated difficult spots, we inched our painful way back along the track.

When we got to the path leading up I really didn't think Alfie was going to make it. I could see how utterly exhausted he was. His feet just shuffled along and it was all he could do to lift his boots over the piles of weed and rocks that littered our way. I climbed closely behind Alfie and placed both my hands on his back. I pushed as he staggered upwards under his burden and our bodies, wedged awkwardly together, fought the pull of gravity and the dying gasps of the storm. And so we managed, eventually, to reach the top.

With a great sob, Alfie lay Louisa on the ground next to the twisted gum tree. The rocks made a shelter from the wind, but now the rain began to fall again. I looked at Louisa. Then I looked at Alfie. Both their faces were white and ghostly. I turned towards the ocean once more. The moon still hung low in the sky and traced a path of wicked brilliance along the heaving back of a monstrous wave that rose from nowhere and rushed towards us. I stood and stared, unable to move, as the sea spilled over the cliff and lapped against my boots.

The lightning began to flash again and there was an enormous crack of thunder. I watched in silence as the lightning struck the twisty gum and the sky filled up with fire.

I opened my eyes. In front of my nose was a piece of mirror. I could see my nose in the mirror. My face was on the floor. The piece of mirror was on the floor. The floor was hard. My head hurt. I tried to move my head. Ouch. I was wet. I was cold and tired. I sat up slowly, holding my head as if I had the world's worst hang-over. Oh my Gawd, as Cherry would say. What on earth had been going on?

Slowly I looked around. I was in the wardrobe van, back on the film set. The full-length mirror lay on the floor, shattered into a million pieces. Wet hair plastered my face. I looked down. I was still wearing the leotard. I began to cry. The costume that symbolised the confused feelings I had about Alfie and Ireland's Circus was torn to shreds. Sequins hung off it and the faded flower sagged limply at my waist. The red leather boots were sodden and the soles ripped and broken. My mind was blank, a bit, fat nothing.

Louisa, Alfie? Oh, God, what was happening? What had happened? How would I ever face Mr Duchesne and The Boss? Kitty Lambert? How would I explain all this? I can't tell them what really happened; they'll think I'm insane.

What to do, what to do? I found my day clothes, stripped, towelled my hair dry and slipped into jeans and a top. I threw the costume and the boots onto the floor amongst the shards of mirror, then threw some other costumes on top of them and poured a jug of water over the lot. I couldn't stop crying. Then, like a vandal, I sneaked out of the van and ran off into the scrub, leaving the depressing mess behind me.

I wandered around in the heat of the early morning for a few hours, not daring to return to the film set. My mind was a jumble of images: Louisa in the cave, the Ireland's big top silent in the afternoon sun, Mrs Ireland cooking dinner, the little kids laughing and playing pirates, Alfie and his sweet, shy kiss. And then the hideous, the gross, the terrible image of Louisa's leotard, *my* leotard, lying torn and dirty on the wardrobe floor.

I didn't know how I could bear it. Once I had calmed down a little I knew I would be able to explain my way out of this mess, somehow, just as I knew beyond any doubt that I would never return to Ireland's

Circus. But worse, much worse, was the thought that I would never see Alfie again.

Chapter 25

It's a long time between getting a mini-series "in the can" and getting it on to the screen. It was hard to remember, sometimes, that I had only just turned sixteen when I landed the role of Louisa Ireland and now, here I was a "grown-up" eighteen and about the attend the gala premier of the *Circus Girl* series.

The cast members had all been flown up to Broome to stay overnight at a Cable Beach resort for the premier at Sun Pictures in China Town. As everybody probably knows, Sun Pictures is the oldest open-air cinema in the Southern Hemisphere and is still going strong. It is a wonderful old place and it is pretty romantic lying back in a deck chair, looking up at a billion stars and watching a movie while the smell of frangipani wafts all around. After the screening there was to be a champagne party at the Sun and dancing to *Scrap Metal*, the hottest band in the Kimberley.

I was quite looking forward to it all but deep down I was really very nervous. I mean, it's one thing to be on a film set where you know everybody, and a different thing entirely to get dressed up to face a whole crowd of strangers and act oh, so cool.

That daggy song, *Just Another Day in Paradise*, kept running through my brain as I got dressed that evening. Broome makes you feel like that. My mum had helped me choose a dress to wear – never thought I'd live to see the day when I'd take fashion advice from Beryl – and I was glad, later, that I had listened to her when I saw what disasters some of the other girls wore. I wasn't totally nerdsville, but I wasn't too in your face, either. I felt like me.

As I sat in front of the bedroom mirror putting on my make-up, I looked hard at my reflection. I looked into my eyes as I so often did these days, and wondered where Louisa Ireland had gone. Was she still in there, somewhere? Would she always be a part of me? There were no answers to the questions I continually asked myself, and I guess there never will be.

I thought, too, about Alfie and how much he had come to mean to me. It was hard to understand how I could have been even just a teeny bit in love with a boy who had lived at the same time as my great-grandfather, but the magic of the short time I spent with Ireland's Circus, and the way I felt whenever I was with Alfie, lingered in my mind. Nostalgia, I guess you could call it, but can you really be nostalgic for something that probably never actually happened?

The first person I saw as my limo pulled up outside Sun Pictures was my friend Cilla. I leaped out and hugged her tightly.

'What on earth are you doing here?'

'Hey, just try and keep me away. You're my best friend – I gotta be here to cheer for you, and, you never know what kind of celebrities we might meet.'

'You never know your luck.' I smiled to myself. Cilla just never changes. 'Hey, are you here by yourself? What, no boyfriend?'

'Uh-hu, not tonight.'

'Whatever happened to that sleazy photographer? He might have been good-looking, but – what a loser.' I thought back to our time in Meekatharra and all that had happened since then.

Cilla giggled, 'A bit of a dude – not.'

Laughing easily and not at all like the cool chicks we were supposed to be, we waltzed into the foyer. I'd been really down when my folks told me they couldn't make it to Broome owing to work commitments, so I was totally rapt to have Cilla there for support. I don't know if I could have done it on my own, but with the truly mental Cilla to distract me I felt I could cope with anything.

Well, almost anything.

The first thing that happened in the foyer was a humungous flash of light as a million (well, half a million) cameras went off. The whole place was crawling with photographers and other media types. Oh my Gawd, as Cherry would have said. In fact, she did. I could see her standing in a corner, pinned against the wall with a glass of champagne in hand and Mrs B yakking non-stop in her ear while Cherry's lips formed the familiar words over and over again. I smiled and waved at the two of them.

Cilla was still attached to my arm. We turned like Tweedle-Dee and Tweedle-Dum and The Boss caught my eye. He pushed towards us through the crowd (where did all these people come from?), his glass of champers held over his head for safety. Mwah! mwah! went the air kisses, but I was truly happy to see him again. It's amazing how close you become to people on a film shoot;

apart from the ones you end up wanting to kill, of course.

There was a sudden hush and Damian Duchesne and his mother swept into the foyer. People rushed forward to welcome them and the night was filled with the sound of lips kissing air. The Boss grabbed my free arm and dragged me, and Cilla, over to The Presence. Don't know why I always thought Mrs Duchesne was such an ogre – tonight she was charming and gracious and seemed eager to chat. Mr Duchesne gave me a big bear hug and muttered congratulatory type noises before moving off into the crowd.

Cilla and I were left standing with Mrs Duchesne. Desperately I tried to think of something to say. Cilla started raving on about nothing, as usual, and easily filled in all the conversational gaps. You could see Mrs Duchesne was quite taken with my mad friend; I was relieved and grateful. Then Mrs Duchesne did that old thing that you do of looking over the shoulder of the person you're talking to and waving to an imaginary friend when you want to get away from a bore at a party. I muttered something and started to move off, but she grabbed my arm.

'No, don't go. There's someone I want you to meet. David – you must meet Bunty.'

'And Cilla,' said my best friend's voice at my elbow.

I turned. The world stood still.

Once again I could feel the rough fleshings of Louisa's costume grip my neck. The noisy, crowded foyer spun around my pounding head. I was back on a cliff-top while the wind and rain howled around and threatened to blow me over the edge. I reached out my hands to Alfie and he grasped them and pulled me towards him. To safety. To a kiss. To ....

'Bunty! My Aunt Maria's told me all these amazing stories about the film shoot, so it's great to meet you at last.'

I opened my eyes. I was, I really was, looking at Alfie. 'D ... David?' I gave a little gasping laugh. 'You – you're David?'

He nodded, and his red hair flopped over his forehead. His green eyes shone with amusement while I continued to stare. Impossible. I looked again. David wasn't exactly like Alfie, there was definitely something different about the nose, but they shared the same colouring and were unmistakably related in some way. I shook my head and looked at Mrs Duchesne. She looked back at me, and then at David.

'Yes, this is David, my eldest sister's great-grandson. Well, I'll leave you young folk to get acquainted. Now, I must find Damian again,' and she toddled off.

'You're related to Mrs Duchesne? But you look like ... What – what was Mrs Duchesne's name before she married?' I knew the answer even as I asked the question.

'Ireland'

'Of course, so that means your great-grandmother, Mrs Duchesne's eldest sister, must have been Louisa Ireland, and – and your great-grandfather was ... don't tell me, I don't believe this ....'

The room swam again as David replied, 'Alfie Warner'.

'Alfie...' My voice cracked. 'Then ... Maria must be little Ria, the youngest of the Ireland kids. Ria, I always thought that was a funny name. But, short for Maria – that explains everything. Well, not everything, but it would explain why she was so keen on getting the mini-series made, and why she was on the set so often. Funny, though, she never had much to do with the production, nothing

to say about how authentic it was, or anything
....'

I thought about the costume and the way it connected me to Louisa's life and I wondered how much Mrs Duchesne knew. I was half talking to myself, half talking to David. He was looking at Cilla. She was talking at him. I felt numb all over.

A bell in the foyer rang and The Boss announced that the screening was about to begin.

Success. Fame. Glamour. These were the things Cilla so desperately wanted. These were the things that seemed to be on offer for me that starry night at the Sun Picture Theatre. But I didn't want them. All I wanted was Alfie, and it seemed I had found him again in David, his great-grandson. So you can imagine how I felt as I watched Cilla and David spend the rest of the evening together, how it hurt to watch them sipping champagne from the same glass, how it squeezed my heart to see them gaze endlessly into each other's eyes.

I left the party early and wandered down to the last street in China Town. I sat on the end of Streeter's Jetty and dangled my legs over the water. The moon was high, but still fat and yellow. Little waves slapped at the pilings. I sniffed, long and deeply. The sharp tang of mangrove swamp filled my nostrils, and I was achingly aware of the first time I had been inside the Ireland's covered wagon with its haunting smell of salt and heat and lantern oil.

I heard the slam of a car door and then footsteps behind me on the wooden planks. I didn't look around until a voice said, 'Bunty ...?' It was David. He held out his hand and pulled me to my feet. Face to face in the moonlight I could see more clearly that he was definitely not Alfie, and yet, and yet ....

'Bun ...'

'Da ...'

'After you,' we said together, then laughed.

There it was again, that familiar bubble of shared laughter.

'Bunty – this will probably sound really, really silly, but I feel like I've met you before. I haven't, have I, somewhere ...?'

Not this time around, I thought, but only managed to say, 'I don't think so. Hey, do you want ....'

'... to go for a coffee?'

We were doing it again, finishing each other's sentences, just like Alfie and I did, once upon a time in a strange else-where. I suppose I should have felt freaked-out but as the situation grew more weird, the happier I felt.

'Um, David, I think there's something you should know. In fact, there are a lot of things you should know about – about me.'

'If it's about you, Bunty, it's bound to be interesting. I did mention Aunt Maria has some great stories, er, about you and the film shoot, didn't I?'

I looked at him sideways. He just laughed and tucked my arm into the crook of his elbow. 'Come on,' he said, 'let's get that coffee.'

We wandered up the jetty towards David's car. Behind us I could hear the rustle of the sea and a little breeze wafted salty smells around us as we walked.

HISTORICAL NOTE

I first had the pleasure and privilege of meeting Evelyn Coverley (nee Alice Evaline Hyland) in 1993 when our family show, Festival Circus, was standing in a lovely park in Matilda Bay on the banks of the Swan River in Peppermint Grove, Perth. One day our overly-large mobile phone rang and a woman, whose name I didn't catch at the time, asked me to phone her mother-in-law who was 95, blind, and recovering from a broken hip. Her mother-in-law, she told me, was an old circus performer who liked to "catch up" with every circus that visited Perth. As she was recovering from an accident she was unable to visit, so *please*, would I ring her? I duly did so, and had a most engaging conversation with the woman who, it turned out, was the pioneering Western Australian circus performer, Alice Evaline Hyland. Thus began an all-too short friendship with a truly remarkable woman and led, eventually, to my writing this novel, based on stories that Ev delighted in telling about her wonderful life.

Alice Evaline was one of 12 children born "on the road" with her father's travelling show, Hyland's Circus. The Hylands were rightly lauded for their acrobatic prowess but were most famous for their astounding horse-training and trick-riding acts. Hyland's Circus began in Queensland and travelled to New Zealand as well as other parts of the colonies at the end of the 19th Century and early 20th Century.

On returning from New Zealand the circus toured South Australia before boarding a sailing ship bound for the Port of Albany. From there the troupe travelled over-land to Perth where they had a marvelous success with a pantomime, complete with artificial water-fall, in Murray Street near Forrest Place. Flush with new costumes, horses and wagons, the family headed for the Eastern Goldfields where, for a time, they abandoned the travelling life and went fossicking for gold, with a small amount of success.

The lure of the circus soon had them on their way again and they headed up to Port Hedland where Mrs Hyland and the younger children embarked on a coastal ship bound for Beagle Bay, north of Broome. The rest of the family travelled over-land, no roads in those days, just miles of sand-hills. Mr Hyland drove a horse and carriage and the older children rode all the way, herding their many beautiful thoroughbred horses.

After a season at the mission in Beagle Bay the Hylands headed down to Broome in time for the luggers to come in with the new harvest of pearls and pearl shell. Cashed-up divers and pearl barons were happy to be entertained by the talented Hyland family and such was their reception that they decided to put down roots by buying the Star Hotel in notorious Sheba Lane on the edge of town. A permanent circus building was erected in the front yard of the pub where the family entertained the pearling community for a number of years.

Tragedy attended this fortune, however, as several of the children, including Ev, became blind owing to Leber Optic Atrophy, a hereditary genetic condition. This did not slow down the indomitable Hylands as, despite this affliction, they continued to perform and entertain.

Evelyn married Aubrey Coverley, the Labor MLA for the Kimberley from 1924 to 1953, and every year travelled all over the electorate with him, first of all on horse-back and then later by T-Model Ford. This was the largest electorate in the world and stretched from the

Far North of WA right down as far as Kalgoorlie and in those early days there were no proper roads, only sandy tracks. The annual trek lasted from November to March, right through the dangers and tribulations of the 'wet season'.

When Evelyn lost her sight she still continued to travel all over the State with her husband. Ev, as she liked to be called, was quick to recognise the benefits of owning a guide-dog and had many faithful companions over the years. When she was in her 80s her current guide-dog died and the powers-that-be decided she was too old to have another one. Undaunted, Ev went off to the dog pound, picked out a likely animal, and trained it herself!

They don't make 'em like that any more.

I have drawn freely on the life of Evelyn to create *Bunty Armitage Circus Girl*. When I told Ev what I was doing she was delighted. Not long before she died she wrote to me, on a very old, battered typewriter, "I rode in the horse races at Halls Creek … you tell them …." I may have taken liberties with Ev's story, but I hope I have captured some of the spirit and atmosphere of those days.

Hyland's Circus is today a largely forgotten, but important, part of Australian circus history in particular and Western Australian history in general. My aim with this novel is to honour the memory of our pioneering circus folk and, especially, the extra-ordinary life of Evelyn Hyland Coverley.

ILLUSTRATIONS

Photographs courtesy of Kerry Freeman,
The Grand Colonial Circus.

Photo of Gerry Robertson by Jacopy.